DATE DUE

DEMCO 25-380

TONY HAWK'S 900 revolution

VOLUME 2

Tony Hawk's 900 Revolution
is published by Stone Arch Books
a Capstone imprint, 151 Good Counsel Drive, P.O. Box 669
Mankato, Minnesota 56002 www.capstonepub.com

Cataloging-in-Publication Data is available on the Library of
Congress website.
ISBN: 978-1-4342-3203-8 (library binding)
ISBN: 978-1-4342-3452-0 (paperback)

Summary: When you skate in New York, it's all about
getting creative, and fourteen-year-old Dylan Crow
considers himself a street artist. You won't catch him
tagging alley walls. Instead, he paints the streets with his
board. He wants to be seen grinding rails in Brooklyn and
popping ollies at the Chelsea Piers. But when Dylan starts
running with the wrong crowd, his future becomes a lot
less certain . . . until he discovers the Revolution.

Photo and Vector Graphics Credits: Shutterstock.
Photo credit page 122, Bart Jones/ Tony Hawk.
Photo credit page 123, Zachary Sherman
Flip Animation Illustrator: Thomas Emery
Colorist: Leonardo Lto

Creative Director: Heather Kindseth
Cover and Interior Graphic Designer: Kay Fraser
Comic Graphic Designer: Brann Garvey
Production Specialist: Michelle Biedscheid

Printed in the United States of America in Stevens Point,
Wisconsin.

032011
006111WZF11

TONY HAWK'S 900 revolution

IMPULSE

BY M. ZACHARY SHERMAN // ILLUSTRATED BY CAIO MAJADO

VOLUME 2

STONE ARCH BOOKS
a capstone imprint

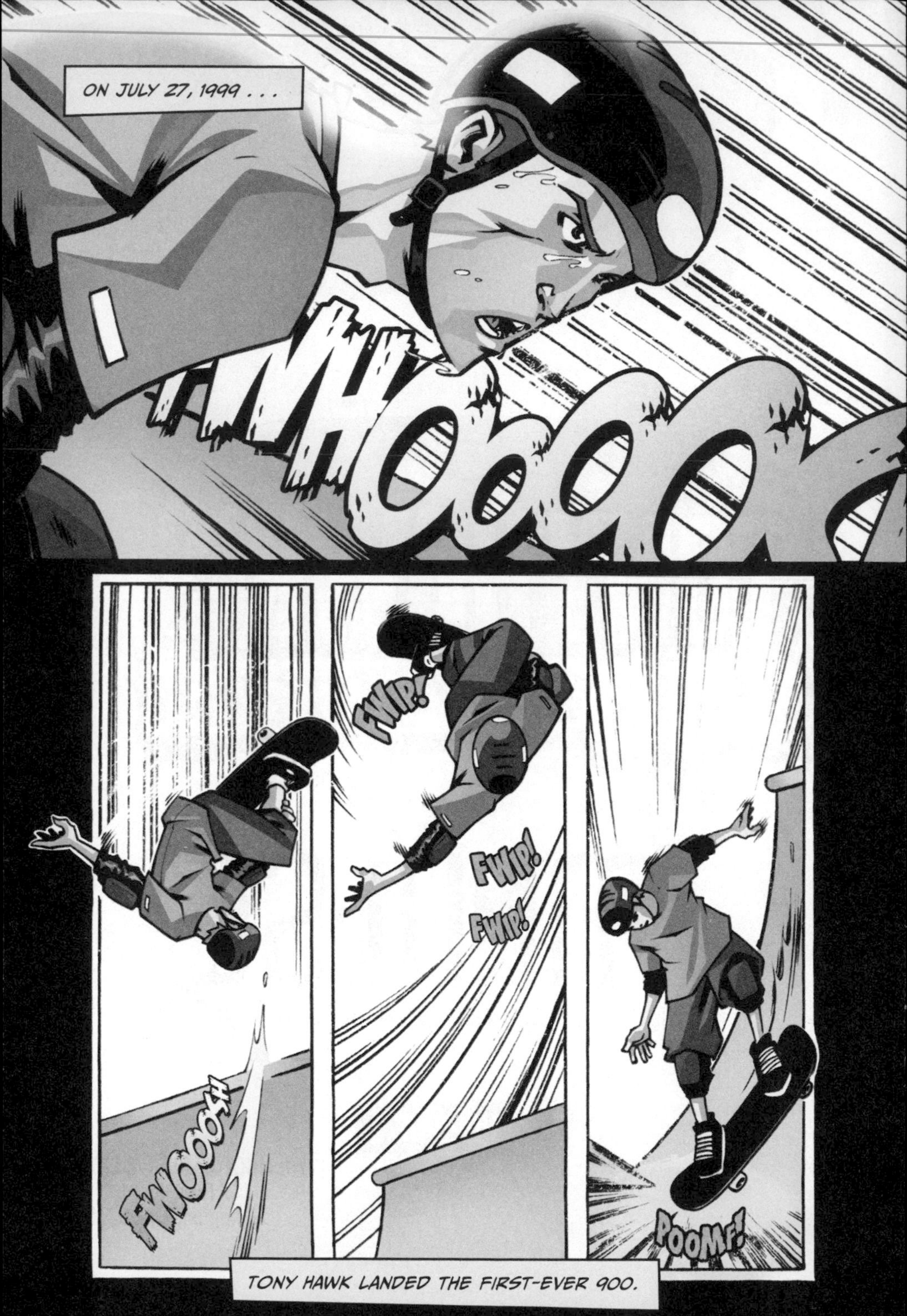
ON JULY 27, 1999 . . .
WHOOO
FWOOOSH
FWIP!
FWIP!
FWIP!
POOMF!
TONY HAWK LANDED THE FIRST-EVER 900.

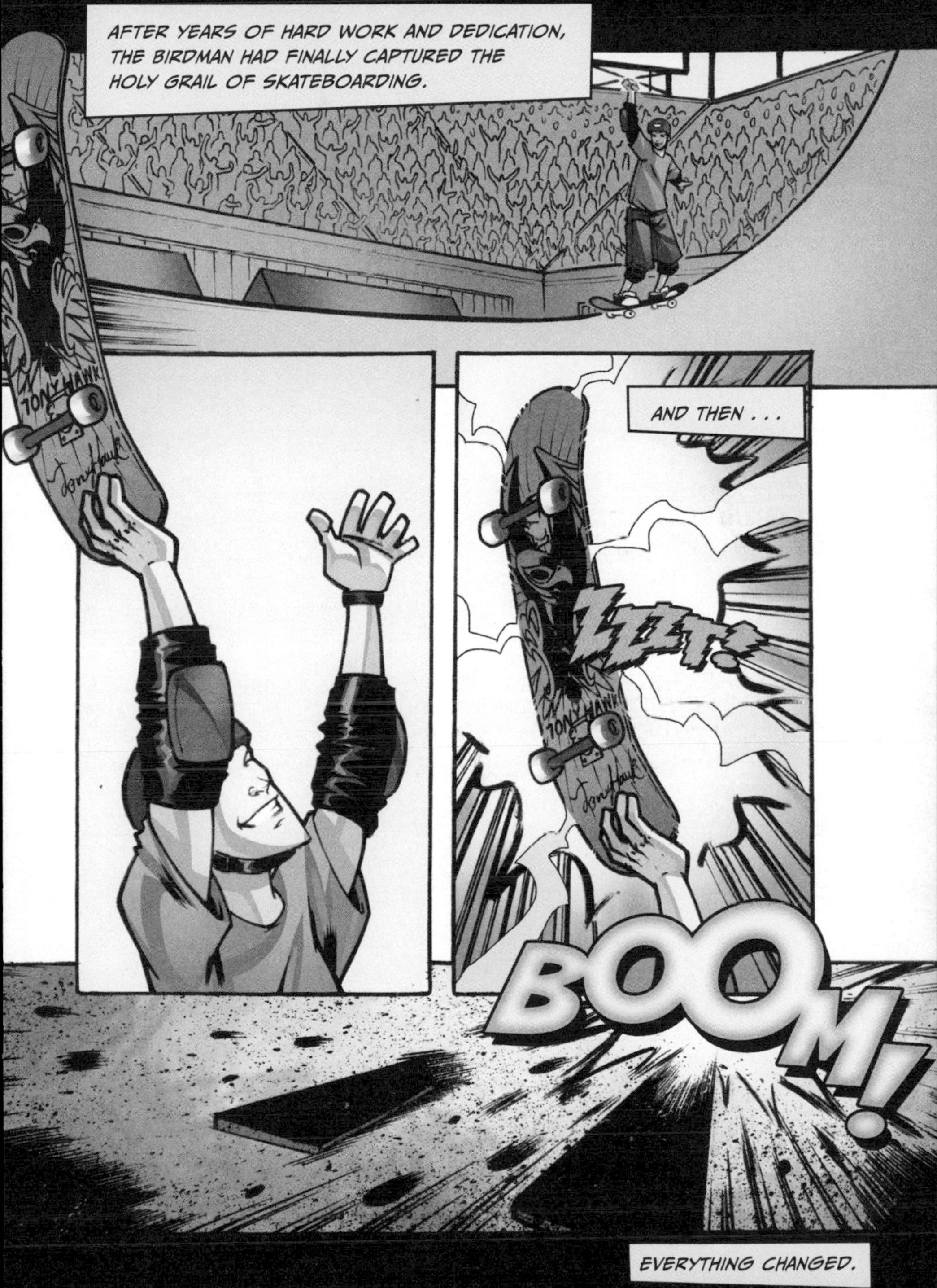
AFTER YEARS OF HARD WORK AND DEDICATION, THE BIRDMAN HAD FINALLY CAPTURED THE HOLY GRAIL OF SKATEBOARDING.
AND THEN . . .
ZZZT!
BOOM!
EVERYTHING CHANGED.

MIKES ADOPTED

KEY TRUST

PAVEMENT NYPD

DECK DYLAN OMAR

DETECTIVE CASE

BLACK HAWK

ENERGY ARTIFACT

1

The shot came fast and silent. It struck the chosen target with maximum force and velocity. A clean hit. Well, as clean as a saliva-drenched spit wad could be.

Thwap! Mr. Greenberg slapped at the back of his neck. He wiped the warm, moist piece of notebook paper from his hairline. The Spanish teacher's nostrils flared. His top lip curled. He spun around from the whiteboard to face his class of freshman students. They had started laughing uncontrollably.

Mr. Greenberg had taught his share of miscreants and class clowns throughout his tenure, but no one quite like —

"Dylan!" the teacher growled, eyeing the young man in the back row of the classroom.

The fourteen-year-old boy looked up without fear.

Dylan's blond hair shadowed most of his face, covering his high cheekbones and strong jaw. "It's Slider, *Señor* Greenberg," he answered.

His name was actually Dylan Crow. The nickname didn't come from his smooth skateboarding moves as Dylan liked to pretend. It came from his ability to slide out of trouble — at least most of the time.

"Not in this class, Mr. Crow," said the teacher. "Besides, I'm more concerned with who shot that spitball at me."

Slider shrugged his shoulders innocently. "Not me," he said, shaking his head. "I would never —"

Just then, a red and white straw fell out of Slider's coat pocket and onto the classroom floor.

"Busted," Mr. Greenberg said with a grin.

Slider stood and nodded, acknowledging his fate.

"Dylan, one of these days you're going to be faced with a decision," the Spanish teacher added. "You're either going to straighten up and do what's right, or you'll continue down this road and crash and burn. It's your choice. Now get out of my classroom!"

As Slider gathered up his books, the girl sitting next to him leaned over. "You're not going to the office, are you?" she whispered.

Slider looked up at her and grinned.

Juliet Malrey.

She was his best friend in the whole world. Smart and fun, not to mention cute. Five feet tall, caramel complexion, and sandy-blond hair that Dylan imagined would feel like the inside of his favorite cotton hoodie.

Slider smiled as he picked up his bag. "I'll meet you at the mall after school," he said.

"How did I know?" she said, returning a smirk.

She was right. At least once a week, Dylan got kicked out of class on purpose. He didn't need a reason to leave.

"Regular place?" she asked.

Slider nodded.

"Try not to get into any more trouble, okay?" Juliet added.

"Hey," said Dylan. "Staying out of trouble is my specialty."

"*Now*, Slider!" Mr. Greenberg barked, holding up the hall pass.

Dylan snatched the paper from the Spanish teacher's hand. He slid out of the classroom and into his element.

A moment later, Slider opened his locker. Inside, his skateboard sat crammed between never-opened textbooks, crumpled sheets of notebook paper, and stacks of detention slips.

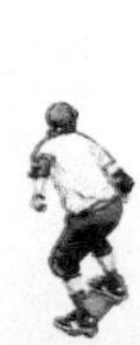

Slider grabbed the front truck of the board between his fingers. He snatched the deck out of the mess.

He threw the board onto the floor, hopped on, and kicked toward the school's front entrance.

"Hasta la vista!" he shouted, speeding past the Spanish classroom, out the school's front exit, and onto the streets of NYC.

*   *   *

Outside, on the rugged concrete, Slider learned all the lessons he needed. Here, he was in total control of everything around him. He was good at this subject. *Really* good.

Dylan had grown up in foster care, popping in and out of other people's lives, never really fitting in with any of them. School was a chore. He had to make new friends every few years — if he was lucky enough to stick it out with a family that long.

At first, Dylan would always try to behave. But eventually he'd screw up somehow, and the family would kick him back into the foster system.

Each family was another roll of the dice. *Maybe this time,* Slider thought. *Maybe I'll actually be with a family that gives a crap.*

Finding a family got harder and harder as he got older. Parents-to-be wanted babies to mold. They didn't want D+ students who shoplifted pastries and broke open parking meters for arcade money.

Besides uncertainty, only one thing had ever been constant in Dylan's life. His foster brother Mikey.

Mikey was older — nearly seventeen — and he looked out for Slider. They'd been placed with the same family several times and formed a bond. If anyone picked on Slider, they had to deal with his big bro.

But Mikey wasn't a good influence on Slider. With several juvenile arrests for shoplifting, petty robbery, and even car boosting, big brother was heading down a bad road.

Slider didn't see it that way. Mikey had always said no one was going to look after them but each other. Together, they needed to scratch and scrape to get by in a world where nobody wanted them.

Dylan slashed in and out of pedestrians on the sidewalk, speeding toward the Game Factory Arcade.

Suddenly, out of nowhere, a police officer stepped right in front of him.

Slider quickly shifted his weight to the left. He circled around the officer, ducking his grasp and shooting off down the street.

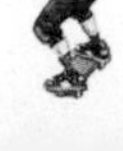

"Watch it!" the cop shouted.

One thing about New York, the curbs were high. Kicktail and an ollie, and he was up in the air.

Time seemed to stop during moments like this one.

The perfect trick.

The perfect hop.

Heaven.

"No skateboarding on the sidewalks, you crazy kid!" the officer yelled after him, but Slider just sped away.

Crazy? thought Dylan. Skateboarding was the one thing he knew for certain.

His only other bit of sanity was Juliet. She was his rock-solid super-friend. Half African American and half Irish, Juliet knew what being stuck in the middle was like. This knowledge was their common bond.

Juliet could read him like a book. No, he wasn't going to the principal's office. He was ditching to go gaming at the arcade.

And he hoped she'd meet him there soon.

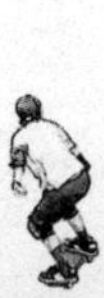

R MIKEY ADOPTE

KEY TRUST

AVEMENT NYP

DECK DYLAN OMA

DETECTIVE CAS

DBLACK HAWK A

ENERGY ARTIFAC

2

"Slider!" came a shout as Dylan entered the Game Factory Arcade at the mall.

"How's it hanging, Jimmy?" replied Slider with a nod.

Jimmy, the arcade's owner, was an old cop. He understood that if kids were ditching in here, they weren't on the streets committing crimes. It was a safe house of sorts. A place where slackers could cut third period without getting the third degree.

Slider carried his board deeper into the black-lit room filled with arcade machines, pinball games, and a gang of kids.

"Hey, you seen my brother around, Jimmy?" he asked, looking across the sea of teens with tokens.

Jimmy nodded his head.

"Yeah, he was here," Jimmy said. "Went downstairs to the Sports Stop, I think."

"Thanks, man," Slider said. "I'll catch you later."

Dylan quickly exited the arcade and hopped on the escalator. Halfway down, he caught a glimpse of Mikey standing near the mall's restrooms.

"Hey," Slider said as he walked over to his brother.

Mikey spun around in shock. "What are you doin' here?!" he snapped. "You following me?"

Slider took a step back. Mikey was nervously fumbling with his watchband, a thick piece of brown leather with a small silver timepiece on it. This was the only memento of his past that Mikey had left. It had belonged to his real father. Mikey never went anywhere without it.

"Whoa, no! Sorry, man," Slider answered quickly. "I just thought you'd be here, that's all."

Mikey shook his head. His eyes darted back and forth around the mall. He appeared to be scanning for someone in particular.

"Sorry, bro, I'm just —" Mikey grabbed Slider by the shoulder. There was something he wanted to tell his brother, but he couldn't get it out.

"What, dude?" asked Slider. "What's wrong?"

"Here," said Mikey, holding out his right hand.

Mikey placed a small silver key into Slider's palm. He closed his brother's fingers tightly around it.

"If I'm right," Mikey continued, "then what I've got going on will set us up for life, brother. *Life.*"

"Uh, okay," said Slider.

"I'm serious," said Mikey, gripping his brother's hand tighter. "No more foster parents. No more system. Just you and me and anything we want. But until then, don't trust anybody and don't let anyone touch this key!"

"What the heck, bro?" Slider objected.

"You take that key to —" but Mikey didn't have time to finish. He spotted something — or someone — in the crowd.

Shoving Slider aside, he nodded toward the escalator. "Go, man! Bolt!" Mikey exclaimed. "Meet me at the house at nine, but do not lose that key. Get me?"

"Sure, no problem," Slider said, backing away.

Slider was more confused than ever. His brother had always been the strong one, the powerful one. Nothing ever shook him. Nothing ever made him nervous. This time he was scared. Really scared. This was no shoplifting gig or boosted car.

What could possibly get Mikey worked up? wondered Slider.

As he ascended the escalator, Slider looked back.

Through the mass of shoppers, Slider spotted a small cloud of people, all dressed in black, approaching Mikey. Three people, all kinds of emo by the look of them, stepped up to his brother and acknowledged him. The tall one looked older, about eighteen, and had a scar that ran the length of his cheek. The younger one with a buzz cut was around his age. The other boy was probably sixteen. But that wasn't the weird thing. What really caught Slider's attention was something else —

They all had skateboards.

A skateboard crew? he thought.

Slider knew every rider in the Five Boroughs, but none of these kids looked familiar. Weirder still, on the shoulder of the oldest boy, a black raven sat quietly. Its talons dug into the kid's leather jacket.

The boys saw Mikey smile and nod over to the exit tunnel. They began to walk out together. Mikey was in the lead and definitely in a hurry. The others took their time, strutting out behind him.

The raven, on the other hand, suddenly turned an eye toward the escalator and looked right in Slider's direction. It detached itself from the taller boy and flew into the air, swooping into the upper floor of the mall. People ducked and moved. The bird flew overhead and finally settled on a trash can at the top of the escalator.

As Slider moved by it, the raven's head flipped to the side, as if it were eyeing him.

Slider stopped, and the two made eye contact.

The bird squawked loudly at him, paused for a beat, and then flew away.

Slider's eyes narrowed as the bird swooped back down onto its owner's shoulder. Then Slider watched them disappear into the darkness.

Weird, Slider thought. He opened his hand and looked down at the silver key glistening in the florescent light overhead. *Very weird.*

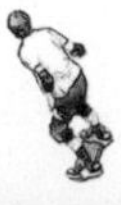

R MIKES HAWPIE
KEY TRUS
AVEMENT NYP
DECK DYLAN OMA
DETECTIVE CAS
DBLACK HAWK A
ENERGY ARTIFAC

3

"Earth to Dylan?" Juliet said. She waved an air hockey paddle in the air and shrugged.

Slider wasn't paying attention. He just stood there in the Game Factory Arcade, totally oblivious. "What?" he finally answered back.

"You're losing? Six to one? One more point, and you owe me a turtle mocha," Juliet said, licking her lips.

"Right," he said. He was lost in thought.

Juliet never beat him at air hockey, but he wasn't thinking about anything other than that raven. It was like it knew Slider had been there, watching them. Like it felt him staring at those boys from across the mall.

Either way, it was getting late, and he needed to be home before curfew. He didn't feel like getting punished. Not again.

Juliet could tell he was distant. "What's the matter?" she asked as she came around the hockey table.

Slider turned and sat on the blue surface. The cool air from the game blew up his back.

"I'm — I'm just worried," he said.

"About Mikey? He'll be okay," replied Juliet.

But he wasn't so sure. Mikey had always been in trouble for one thing or another, but this time felt different to Slider. Mikey never ran with anyone. He was a loner. And those other guys all looked . . . creepy.

"Maybe they were vampires!" Juliet joked.

"What?" he asked.

"You know, maybe they're trying to lure him in with their sexy, animalistic vampire powers so they can suck his blood!" she said with a smile.

Slider never felt like he had to be anything other than himself around Juliet. No walls. No fake macho attitude. He could be himself because she liked him for who he was and that made him feel comfortable around her. He could be fourteen and not have to act eighteen.

Slider looked up at her and started laughing. "Vampire?" he said. "Juliet, way too many romantic vampire movies for you, goofball!"

Slider gazed up at the clock — 8:03 pm. "Come on, let's jet," he said.

*   *   *

As they exited, they saw that the sun was gone. The moon was rising, casting a silver glow on the city that never slept.

They hit the pavement. Slider's composite wheels crunched on the sidewalk as Juliet's skateboard echoed closely behind. They got about half a block away when they noticed a crowd gathering at the end of the street. Flashing police lights bathed the area in red and blue colors as they oscillated back and forth against the buildings.

Slider's eyes got wide. A knot began growing in his throat.

"Wow!" Juliet said, grinding to a halt. "Let's see what's happening."

"No!" Slider started, but she grabbed his arm and pulled him toward the officers.

As Juliet and Slider got closer, they curved and weaved through the crowd until they reached the front. They ducked under the yellow and black plastic tape that secured the entire area.

The scene was like something out of a movie. The area was cordoned off with plastic police streamers. NYPD squad cars and patrolmen attempted to keep the crowds at bay.

Policemen and Crime Scene Investigators looked for clues and spoke with witnesses as they processed the area. Flash bulbs went off as several techs took pictures. One CSI squatted down and snapped a shot of what looked like a black feather, and then placed it in a paper evidence bag with a gloved hand.

Looking up, Slider heard a man speaking.

"And then what did you see?" an older detective asked a young woman. They stood near enough to Slider and Juliet for them to hear clearly.

"The older kid was roughing up the other one pretty bad," the woman said. She looked over to where the event had taken place. "He tried to fight back but couldn't, you know? He didn't have a chance against all three of them."

"I wonder who it was?" Juliet asked.

Slider craned his neck to see. But at that instant, he got an empty feeling in the pit of his stomach. He watched as another crime scene tech bent down to retrieve something from behind a trash bin.

It was a brown leather band with a small silver watch on it . . .

"Mikey's watch."

Slider's eyes went wide. He turned and ran, leaving Juliet alone in the crowd.

"Slider! Where are you going?" she yelled after him.

It was too late. He was well out of range of her voice and heading into the night on his skateboard.

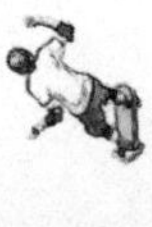

SLIVE
SE JULIE
EW YORK CIT
R MIKEY ADOPTE
W KEY TRUST
AVEMENT NYP
DECK DYLAN OMA
DETECTIVE CAS
DBLACK HAWK A
A ENERGY ARTIFAC

4

Less than a block away, Slider could see the pulsating red and blue lights covering his street in color. As he approached the small brownstone he called home, his heart began to race. He watched cops move in and out of his own front door.

He kicked faster as he neared the same yellow and black tape that blocked off the crime scene at the mall. He ducked under it, dropped his skateboard, and bolted toward the front door.

The perimeter officer did a double take as the 14-year-old rocket whooshed by him in a blur. "Hey — Hey! Somebody stop that kid!"

On the top of the front steps stood a young detective. The man was about thirty five with short brown hair and a strong build.

He was speaking with another officer as Slider approached him like a bullet.

The detective reached out and grabbed the young man by the arm.

Slider fought to break his grasp.

"And where do you think you're going, kid?" asked the detective. Three uniformed cops rushed up the stairs, ready to take Slider into custody.

Trying his best to hold back his tears, Slider yelled out. "This is my house! I live here!"

"You're the brother . . ." the detective said softly.

Flashing a look at the other officers, Detective David Case shook his head "no" and nodded for them to back off. The cops turned and retreated down the stairs.

"Trust me, kid," Detective Case said. "You don't want to go in there." The sincerity in his voice was mixed with a concern for the young man's well-being.

Slider could sense it. He stopped struggling and pointed to the front door. "But, Jeannine and Benny?" he asked, afraid of the answer he was going to get.

Detective Case let go of Slider's arm, releasing the young man. "Your foster parents, they — um, they're gone."

"What do you mean, 'gone'?!" shouted Slider, fear pulsing through his brain.

"Sorry, poor choice of words," said the detective. "They're on their way to the hospital. They were beaten pretty badly. Looks like a home invasion."

"Are they —?" Slider stammered.

The detective shook his head. "No, they're fighters. They're tough," he said. "Your foster dad, he called us after the assailants left. The EMTs got them stabilized. Do you have any idea who would want to do this?"

"No. No!" Slider shot back. Tears welled up in his eyes, and he tried desperately to be strong, not to cry.

Detective Case put a hand on the teen's back. He led him down the stairs. "Come on, let's go somewhere and talk, okay?" he said.

Not wanting to speak, Slider nodded and walked off with the detective.

Down the street, separated from the commotion, a sleek midnight-black 1959 Ford 100 truck sat near the curb, unnoticed by anyone. Suddenly, its lights flashed on and its engine purred to life, powering up to follow the pair.

"Funny thing is," the detective started, "I have an APB out on you right now. Then you just show up right in my lap."

The neighborhood around the corner from Slider's house was always brighter and livelier than his block.

This was mostly due to the fact that the dance clubs were open 24 hours in this part of the city. Traffic was constantly moving through the neighborhood.

New York was different than most cities. On one block, you could have nightlife and mayhem, but right around the corner, total family neighborhoods. Strangely enough, the two never really seemed to clash. But hard economic times were forcing crime from one part of the city to overflow into other parts that no one had ever expected.

Had that been what happened to Slider's house? His foster parents? Had someone from their own neighborhood done this?

Luckily for Detective Case, this late-night activity also meant the 24-hour diners were open. It gave him a place he could take Slider away from the crime scene so they could speak without distraction.

Inside Big Rick's Burger Joint, Slider sat at a table, his skateboard at his side. Detective Case waited for their food at the counter.

Soon, Case returned to the table with a burger and fries for the kid. A hot dog for himself.

"Why?" Slider asked.

"It's just procedure," Case answered. "We have to find the other members of the family."

"Why?" Slider asked again.

"To make sure they're okay," Case replied sloppily, his mouth full of an all-beef frank and bun.

Slider frowned. "I was at the mall all night with a friend. You can rule me out," he said.

Case swallowed hard. "As what? A suspect?" asked the detective. "Look, kid, I saw how you reacted to what happened. That was genuine. I know you ain't got nothing to do with this crime."

"Then what?" asked Slider.

The detective smiled. "What can you tell me about your brother?" he asked, stuffing another bit of spiced dog in his mouth.

"You've got his record," Slider hammered back. "Look for yourself."

"Slider —" Case started. His tone sounded honest.

Looking up, Dylan's defenses started to lower. No adult ever called him Slider. *Ever.* Not even his foster parents. More importantly, how did this detective know his nickname?

"I don't care about his record," the detective continued. "To me, he's a victim. Your foster parents are victims. I just want to bag the people that hurt them, get your brother back, and make sure you're safe. So, what can you tell me?"

Slider wasn't sure what to think. Was this guy for real? He'd seen cop shows on TV and knew their tactics: get the guy to like you right before you lock him up.

Slider hadn't done anything wrong. Maybe he should trust this guy. He seemed nice enough, but then Mikey's words echoed through his head —

"Don't trust anybody."

"No, sorry," Slider answered softly, looking away.

The detective's eyes narrowed. He took a french fry and pointed it at Slider. "Kid, I'm doing everything I can to be patient here," he said. "I've got a major assault and kidnapping on the west side and a home invasion in the avenues that seem to be connected. You know what the only common link is?"

Slider shook his head.

"You," answered the detective.

"Hey, look, man," said Slider. "Mikey was my brother. He looked out for me."

"He was a criminal," Case replied. "Sure, he was a low-level crook. He lifted stereos, TVs, stuff like that. Not good, but not as bad as drugs or murder. The way it looks to me? He ripped off the wrong guys — stiffed them or something — so they took him out. Then they came looking for whatever they'd hired him to steal at your place. Your parents just got in the way."

Slider thought about that. Those dudes. It must have been those guys at the mall. It must have been.

"He went missing two hours before the home invasion, and we have no leads on whoever did this," continued the detective. "As far as I can see, whoever took your brother is going to come looking for you."

Slider stood and picked up his board.

"Nice deck," Case said, pointing at Slider's skateboard.

"What d'you know, grandpa?" asked Slider.

"I used to skate back in the day," Case replied.

"Poser."

Reaching into his coat, Case removed a business card and handed it to Slider. "If you think of anything, call me," he said.

Slider took it as Case stood.

"Where are you going?" Slider asked.

"I'm taking you to juvenile services," said Case.

"Oh, no! No way!" Slider pushed the man back, ran for the front exit, and rushed out the glass doors.

The deck hit the street. The young man kicked hard, leaving Big Rick's Burger, and Detective Case, behind in a New York minute.

Case smiled. He picked up the basket of burger and fries and called to the waiter, "I'll get this to go."

MIKEY ADOPTED

KEY TRUST

DECK DYLAN

DETECTIVE

BLACK HAWK

ENERGY

5

Swoosh. Slam. Swoosh. Slam.

The lock on the gate was old and rusted and never really held all that well anyway. It was easy to jimmy open. The chain-link fence that surrounded the skate park was only about seven feet tall, but Slider hadn't felt like climbing it.

Swoosh. Slam. Swoosh. Slam.

He took out his pain and anger on the bowls, ramps, and half-pipes at the skate park. Here, he could clear his head of frustrations and emotions without anyone else around. So into the empty concrete pools he went. He popped up and rocketed into turns and flips. He even executed an ollie finger flip on the verty — anything he could do to get the aggression out.

Swoosh. Slam. Swoosh. Slam.

But, as all good runs do, this one ended as Slider popped out of the bowl. He landed at the lip, pressing down on his front grip tape on the deck to roll out.

A spotlight of white light shined down from one of the three lamps that surrounded the park. Outside that glowing cone, there was little but darkness. The trees of the park hid the city well.

Stopping next to a bench, Slider removed his helmet and kneepads. Then, a squawking noise pulled his eyes upward. Perched on one of the lampposts, a raven sat watching.

The image took a second to register, but then Slider's eyes went wide. Was this the same bird that was in the mall earlier that day? The one that had been watching him?

Slider pressed down on the tail of his board. It flipped up toward his outstretched hand.

Just then, something shot out of the darkness and grabbed the front truck, ripping the board away from Slider. It, too, disappeared from under the white-hot spotlight and into the dark.

"Nice board," a low, male voice rumbled from the darkness.

Eyes squinting, Slider could barely make out a shape as, above him, the raven's cawing got louder.

"Thanks," Slider answered back nervously.

Finally, out of the blackness, a person emerged. It was the oldest of the kids who had met with his brother that day.

"You're good, kid. Really good. Too good, actually," the boy said, circling Slider and looking him up and down. He ran the skateboard over in his hands, examining it, as if he were looking at some piece of alien technology.

"But it ain't because of this piece of junk," he said. "I'm Rodney, by the way."

"Do I know you?" Slider asked.

A big smile crept over Rodney's face as he slowly shook his head. "No, but I know you. I've been looking for you. For *it*."

It, Slider thought. *What 'it'?*

"Give me my board back," Slider demanded as the young man continued circling and sizing him up and down.

"Here —" Rodney said, tossing the board back. "It's not what I'm looking for anyway, and you know it."

Catching it, Slider spun, trying to keep eye contact with Rodney the entire time. Fear and anger built inside of him. Was this the guy? Did he hurt his brother? What did he want now?

"Where's my brother?" Slider yelled.

Rodney stopped grinning. With the light of the lamp glaring down on him, his eyes went black. His features became menacing and evil.

"Mikey's gone," Rodney said. "He abandoned you."

"He'd never — where, where to?" Slider asked, but Rodney didn't care.

"Ha! I'll answer one of your questions if you answer one of mine," proposed Rodney.

"Fine. Did you kill him?" Slider asked.

Rodney shook his head. "Nah, not my style. I gave him a beat-down, but he was breathing when we left him. My turn. Those moves — they your own?" he asked.

Slider nodded. "Yeah . . ."

Tilting his head to the side, the boy's eyes narrowed. He didn't believe him.

"No, they're not. Where is it? You have it on you, don't you?" Rodney asked.

"Where's what?"

Confused, Slider took a step back, looking for an out. He immediately bumped into another person. Startled, he jumped back and turned.

That's when he saw him.

Standing there was one of the other kids from the mall. The kid with the buzz-cut. He cracked the knuckles on his right hand.

"Don't worry, Buzzer won't hurt you," Rodney said. "Unless I tell him to."

Slider had a very bad feeling about this entire situation. He was a heck of a skateboarder, but in no way was he a fighter. Mikey had been that for both of them. If these were in fact the kids that had something to do with Mikey's disappearance, what could he do? What chance did he have?

"Now, where's the Artifact?" Rodney shouted.

Slider was confused. He didn't know what Rodney was talking about.

"The what?!" asked Slider.

"The Artifact!"

"What?" Slider repeated.

"The piece your brother gave you that he was supposed to give me!" Rodney yelled.

"Dude!" Slider yelled. "I don't know what you're talking about."

Raising his hand, Rodney snapped his fingers. Suddenly, the kid behind Slider grabbed his arms. The skateboard dropped to the ground near his feet. Rodney approached him.

Right in front of him now, Rodney pointed a finger in Slider's face. "Listen to me, kid. I'm gonna ask you one more time —"

In a flash, Slider stomped down, flipping the tail of his board with the full weight of his foot. Rocketing up, the front of the deck smashed into Rodney's crotch, hitting him square in the family jewels.

Slamming his head back as hard as he could, Slider whacked the other kid in the nose with the rear of his skull. Buzzer yelped in pain and quickly released his captor.

This was his chance! As Slider stepped on the board and pushed off, something entered his mind: there were three of these guys at the mall . . . weren't there?

"Twitch!" Rodney yelled as he bent at the waist, trying to catch his breath.

Out of the blackness, the third teen appeared and threw a right cross at Slider's head.

Ducking, Slider grabbed the side of his board and leaned to his right. The punch missed by mere inches.

But the turn was too great, and he was headed right for the bowl. In the next instant, he was in the empty pool, but to his delight, his momentum shot him up and out faster than he'd ever ridden before.

Slider rocketed over the lip and high into the air. So high, in fact, he flew over the retaining fence!

Recovering from his groin-shot, Rodney stood up in time to see Slider glide to freedom.

"Get that punk!" he shouted as Slider landed the jump perfectly.

"Own moves! Yeah right," Rodney said. The goons grabbed their own boards and took off after Slider.

The chase was on! Kicking with his entire might, Slider maneuvered through the maze of walkways in Central Park. The two teens followed close behind him.

With no time to think about why they were chasing him, all Slider could do was to stay ahead of them. He crouched and kicked as fast as he could, but they were gaining.

Looking forward, Slider smiled. Up ahead was something that might help.

The area was littered with rest stops where pedestrians and park visitors could sit and watch the birds or just enjoy the natural surroundings. Each stop had a bench, a trash can, and a lamppost that illuminated the area at night. Most of the time, the benches and the trash cans were secured to the post with a heavy chain and a massive padlock. The security kept anyone from stealing or moving them.

Slider sped up on one of these spots and noticed a bench and trash can that weren't locked to their adjoining lamppost.

Desperately, he kicked out, knocking the bench over. It tumbled over and turned, completely blocking the path.

But the other teens just smiled and shook their heads as they approached the roadblock.

Buzzer did a pop and shove, clearing the bench by an inch. Twitch flew way over it, pulling the highest boneless finger flip Slider had ever seen!

Slider turned left, down through the dark part of the park. His eyes went wide as a massive stone staircase met his gaze. In an instant, he ollied up, turned his board 90-degrees to the metal handrail, and did a boardslide down the banister. Weight forward, Slider breathed heavily as he anticipated his dismount. His wheels slammed to the concrete hard, but he didn't falter. He was good. He was really, really good.

But the other boys? They were better.

One launched straight out over the staircase, right into the air, and landed thirty feet below.

The other boy did a boardslide as well, but only the tail of his board connected with the metal handrail. His balance was perfect.

Slider watched in amazement as the boys kept coming.

How?! he thought. *That's impossible!*

Finally, they were right next to him.

Buzzer reached out, trying to grab him. Slider kept moving, ducking and weaving as the hands missed him by mere inches.

Twitch pulled a baseball bat out of a small leather holster sewn into his jacket. He started swinging it at Slider's head.

"Whoa!" Slider yelped as the bat swished right by his face.

Ahead of them, the path was getting narrower as they neared the exit to the park. The lights and sounds of the city were returning as they skated faster toward the gate.

Head down and eyes closed, Slider desperately pushed off and kicked as hard as he could.

Like a missile, Slider shot out of the park entrance and flew right into traffic.

Luckily, Friday nights on 5th Avenue were jam-packed with taxis and people trying to take advantage of the coming weekend. He avoided most of the traffic, but a bright yellow taxi was now blocking his path of escape.

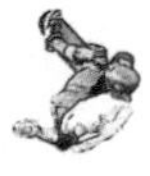

Without a second to spare, Slider planted his weight backward and oriented the board nose out. He executed a laser heel flip turn, coming to an almost complete 90-degree turn as the cab swerved toward the park opening.

The cab spun left, just as the other two boys came soaring out of the park exit. Unable to stop, they both skated into the side of the cab. They flipped over the hood of the car and crashed to the street.

Standing upright, both boys looked at each other and shook their heads, dazed, but amazed they were alive.

"Look what you did you my cab!" the cabbie said as he leaned out the window and saw the dent in the side.

"Shut up!" Buzzer yelled, searching for his board.

"Where's my board?" Twitch moaned.

"Bad news, bro . . ." Buzzer said as he reached down and picked up what was left of Twitch's board. The front truck had ripped away from the wood and was dangling by a splinter.

"Where's mine?" Buzzer said, looking around. As Buzzer searched for his board, he found it just in time to watch it get run over by a truck. It was smashed into kindling.

About half a block down, Slider stopped, breathing heavily.

His board in his hand, Slider smiled. The two boys were now out of commission.

Suddenly, a pair of headlights lit him up. As he turned, the smile fell off his face.

He leaped out of the way just as Rodney's truck barreled down on him. It popped the curb and smashed into a trash can, sending litter flying over the hood and over the windshield.

Clacking his board on the ground, Slider sailed down the road. Turning left, out of traffic, he busted onto another side street.

Rodney saw him cut right. He stopped the truck and leaned out the window, waving at Twitch and Buzzer.

"Get in!" Rodney ordered.

The truck sped off as the two teens hopped into the bed and slapped the sides. Tires kicked up smoke on the pavement. Rodney peeled out and pulled a left, heading toward Slider.

"You can't kill him, Rodney! We don't have it yet!" Twitch yelled over the rushing wind.

"Yeah, well, I can sure as heck hurt him!" Rodney shot back.

On Riley Street, Slider stopped and looked behind him. Shooting through the intersection, Rodney and his gang raced toward him at highspeed.

The truck was just about to hit him. Slider kicked out into the street. He grabbed on to the back end of a taxi as it sped by, catapulting him forward.

The truck just missed him by inches. The taxi kept moving down Riley Street, toward an intersection up ahead.

Making a quick reverse and turn, Rodney was in hot pursuit.

But to Slider's dismay, the light ahead at the intersection turned red. His taxi tow-car stopped.

Slider looked back.

Rodney was seconds away from making Slider the meat in a bumper sandwich.

"Latch on!"

Slider's head snapped to the left to see Detective Case's car, driving in the opposite direction!

In a heartbeat, Slider kicked over to Case's rear bumper. He grabbed on, and they were off, accelerating away from the thugs.

The other boys watched Case and Slider drive right by them. For a moment, Rodney took his eyes off the road in surprise.

The sound of crumpling metal came from far behind Slider. He heard it clearly. Rodney's truck had rear-ended the car at the stoplight.

The other driver emerged, screaming and yelling as Rodney got out of the truck's cab. Oblivious to the man's ranting and raving, he turned and watched as Slider, still hanging on to the back bumper of Detective Case's car, sped around a corner.

"This ain't over . . ." he mumbled.

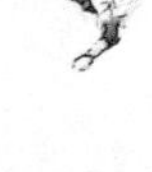

SLIDE
& JULIET
NEW YORK CIT
R MIKEY ADOPTED
U KEY TRUST
PAVEMENT NYP
DECK DYLAN OMA
DETECTIVE CAS
D BLACK HAWK A
ENERGY ARTIFAC

6

"How did I know where you were? Kid . . ." Case said as he shoveled the chili-cheese dog in his face and spoke with his mouth full. "I'm a detective!"

Slider winced. A single bean attached to a piece of cheese slipped from Case's lip and stuck on his chin.

"Dude, you're disgusting," Slider moaned.

"And you're never hungry! Don't you eat?" Case said. He picked at Slider's fries as they sat in Roy's once again. The place was deserted. They were the only ones in the room.

"Not when you do. It makes my stomach turn," Slider replied.

"Bwahahaha!" Case laughed, the dangling bean shaking on his chin from a cheesy bungee cord on a tiny bridge.

Slider handed Case a napkin and motioned at his chin. "Seriously, dude," he said. "We're in public."

Wiping his chin, Case put the napkin down and pointed at Slider as he chewed.

"Now do you believe me?"

Slider nodded as he looked away at the floor.

"Did they say what they wanted?" Case asked.

"Yeah," Slider began. He didn't know who to trust.

"Look, Slider, I really am trying to help you here," Case pleaded.

"I know, I just — Mikey said not to trust anyone."

"And where is he now?" Case asked coldly.

He looked up at the detective. He knew Case was right. He had to trust someone — someone older than himself.

"They were looking for something called the 'Artifact,'" Slider said finally as he reached for a fry.

Case stopped chewing. His face went completely white.

Slider did a double take from the fries to the detective. "Do you need the Heimlich or something, man? You okay?" he asked.

"Do you know where it is?" Case asked softly.

"Nope," he said, taking his first bite of food. "Don't even know what they're talkin' about. Do you?"

Slowly, Case leaned across the table. He looked Slider dead in the eye.

"If you have any clue where this thing is — even an inkling — I need you to tell me," Case said softly.

"Why? What is it?"

"Well," Case began, "if it's what I think it is, then there's a lot more at stake than I thought."

"But *why*?" Slider repeated.

"*Why* doesn't matter — the important question is *'where.'* Obviously, they're looking for this Artifact, and they think you have it."

"Dude, seriously, what is this Artifact?" Slider asked.

"You really want to know?"

"Yes! Please!" Slider answered back.

"I'm not exactly sure . . . but I know people will kill for it," he answered.

"My brother —?"

"I think he had it and was going to sell it to those kids. But he must have tried to bribe them for more money or something," Case said.

"And who are those kids?" he asked.

"I don't know. I caught a pic of one of them with my cell as we drove by, and uploaded it to the central database. They're running a facial analysis now, and trying to ID him."

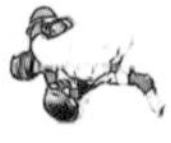

"That's very *CSI* of you," Slider said with a smile.

Case took another bite of his hot dog and swallowed.

"You know what it is and you're not telling me, don't you?" Slider asked.

"I *can't* tell you," added Case. "If it is what I think it is, it's dangerous, and you need to stay out of this."

"I can't believe this. What is this thing?!" Slider exclaimed.

"Something no one can control," Case answered.

"Whatever," Slider said. He stood and grabbed his board. Case made no move to stop him.

"Aren't you going to try and take me in?" Slider asked suspiciously.

Case shook his head. "Won't do any of us any good," he answered. "But if you need me, call me. I can help you."

"Help?" began Slider.

Mikey was gone.

The world had changed.

Nothing would ever be the same.

"The only person that can help me is *me*," he added.

And with that, Slider walked out the door.

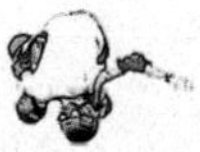

SLIDE
JULIET
NEW YORK CITY
MIKEY ADOPTED
KEY TRUST
MOVEMENT NYP
DECK DYLAN OMA
DETECTIVE CAS
DBLACK HAWK A
ENERGY ARTIFAC

Awakened from a twilight sleep, Juliet looked at her bedroom window. A small pebble flew into it and lightly tapped on the glass. The clock read almost three in the morning when she rose to investigate the mysterious noise.

Pulling the curtains back, Juliet saw Slider standing on the front lawn.

He bent over and picked up another small rock, not noticing her at the window. As he threw it, Juliet opened the panel of glass and leaned out. The pebble pelted her square in the forehead.

"Slider!" yelled Juliet.

"Oh, man! Sorry!" he whispered.

"I'll be right down." She closed the window.

"Are you sure this is okay?" Slider asked quietly as Juliet opened the back door to the house.

"Yeah, just be quiet. My parents are in Florida for the weekend, and Jenny's with her boyfriend in the living room 'watching a movie'."

"I just don't want to get you into trouble," he said softly.

"No one'll know," she assured him. "Come on."

They walked through the back of the house quietly. Then they climbed the stairs toward the second story and the family bedrooms.

"So are you going to tell me?" she asked, opening the guest room door.

"Tell you what?" questioned Slider.

The room was dark, lit only by a single lamp by the side of the bed. That didn't matter. Slider was so tired that he only noticed the cushy pillows.

"What's going on and why you bolted from the mall tonight?" she answered.

Slider hesitated for a second and then looked up at her. His eyes filled with confusion. Juliet was smart and very quick. If there was anyone he could trust, it was her.

Maybe she could help him put it all in perspective.

"Mikey's gone missing, and my foster parents are in the hospital," he said softly.

"Oh my gosh! What happened?!" she said, sitting next to him on the bed.

"I dunno . . . But, tonight, at the mall? When the cops were there?" he started.

"Yeah?"

"I took off because they found Mikey's watch at the scene."

"The leather gauntlet one?" Juliet asked.

Slider nodded. "Yeah, the watch was at the scene of the crime," he said. "I saw it."

"Whoa. Is your brother okay?" she asked.

"He's missing. And then I went home, and the cops were there, too! They told me my foster parents were hurt in a break-in. The crooks were looking for something, and my foster parents tried to stop them."

"What were they looking for?"

Slider reached into his pocket.

"Before he disappeared, Mikey gave me a key. This key." He pulled the small silver key out of his pocket and looked at it. "I think those thugs want what's locked inside of — well, whatever this key opens."

"I know what it opens," Juliet said, staring at the key.

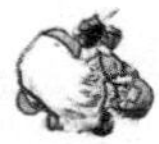

Slider stared at her. "You do?"

"Sure," Juliet answered. "That's a locker key."

"It is?" Slider was confused.

"Yeah, for the Skate-O-Rama on 23rd and Grant," she added. "My mom use to take me there for my ice skating lessons every Thursday after school."

"No way . . ." Slider said, looking at the key. "Whatever those kids want, it's in that locker. I have to go!"

As Slider rose to leave, Juliet placed a hand on his chest and stopped him.

"Wait, what kids?" she asked.

"Like I told you — three older kids. They were talking with Mikey before he disappeared. They chased me through the park and tried to beat me up," he said.

"What?" she said excitedly. "Did you tell the cops?"

Slider was silent, knowing his answer was going to upset her.

"Yeah, but not about the key," he replied.

"Dylan . . ." she said with a sigh.

"Mikey said not to trust anyone!"

"So why are you telling me?" she said.

"You're different!" Slider tried to explain. "And this one cop — a detective — he's pretty cool, but I'm still not sure I can trust him."

"Slider, it's three in the morning," said Juliet. "Trust me. The skating rink is closed. They open at eleven on Saturdays. We can take the subway and get there right when the doors open."

"We?" he said with a smile.

"Yeah, we," Juliet said, pulling the blanket down for him. As he fell backward onto the covers, Slider looked up at her with tired, heavy eyes.

"Juliet, why are you so nice to me?" he asked softly.

"Because, you know —" she stammered.

He shook his head.

"Because, you're my friend, Dylan . . ." she said, pushing her curly bangs away from her eyes.

Is she flirting with me? Slider wondered. Girls didn't normally enter into Slider's world. He was never really around in one place long enough to get close to anyone.

But there was something about Juliet's smile. Something that made him feel safe. It was a feeling he only had when he was skating — a security and a sense of internal power. It made him feel like he was ready to take on the whole world. He wasn't sure what it was or why, but Juliet's kindness gave him strength.

In Juliet's mind, Slider was dynamic, daring — all the qualities she was missing in her life. Being with him made her feel adventurous.

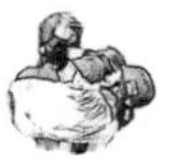

That, and he was really cute.

"Oh man, this bed is soft," Slider said as he took off his sneakers and readied to climb into the covers.

Juliet walked to the doorway. "'Night," she said with a shy glance.

"'Night. And Juliet —?" Slider began.

"Yeah?" she said as she stopped.

"Thanks."

SLIDE
JULIE
NEW YORK CIT
R MIKEY ADOPTE
KEY TRUS
VEMENT NYP
DECK DYLAN OMA
DETECTIVE CAS
D BLACK HAWK A
R ENERGY ARTIFAC

8

The Skate-O-Rama was open by the time Slider and Juliet got to the rink. It had been open early for hockey practice, as several of the amateur leagues used the ice for skirmishes and run-throughs.

Two teams were just finishing as Juliet and Slider walked inside. Some of their gear was left on the benches as the players moved toward the locker rooms at the far end of the building.

"It's cold in here," Slider said.

"Duh, it's an ice skating rink?" Juliet replied.

The building was an enormous metal warehouse that housed an ice skating rink in the center of the room. The ice was encased in retaining walls, or hockey boards, with Plexiglas windows.

The rink had four entrances onto the ice: two side doors that lead to the team benches and the side exits, and the larger Zamboni entrances on either end of the ice.

Metal bleachers flanked the rink for spectators. However, today, they were empty.

On the far side of the room, opposite the front door, a bank of metal lockers sat nestled between the doorways to the restrooms.

"There!" Slider said as he pointed across the ice to the lockers.

After running around the perimeter past the bleachers, Slider looked at the key. Two small numbers were engraved on it: 09. Slider hunted for the same number on the front of the lockers.

"Here —" Juliet said. She tapped on a small, metal door that was about chest high.

Placing the key in the lock, Slider stopped suddenly. His face filled with concern.

Juliet looked at him. "What is it? What's wrong?" she asked.

"What if —" he started, but quickly stopped. He chose his next words very carefully.

"What if what's inside here isn't meant to be found?" Slider said quietly.

"We already found it," Juliet replied.

"No, I mean what if we aren't supposed to find it," Slider continued. "A lot of people around me have already been hurt over whatever's in here. Maybe I'm just supposed to let it stay lost?"

"Yeah, well, problem with that is, they empty out these lockers every other day," said Juliet. "I should know. I lost a pair of skates leaving them here once." She reached over and took Slider's hand in hers. "Someone's gonna find it. Better you than those guys you were talking about."

Slider smiled, and they turned the key together.

The teens closed their eyes and winced as they pulled together. The small, gray door opened with a metallic creak.

There was no sound, no rush of air, no explosion, no anything.

Opening one eye, Slider peeked inside the miniature metal locker.

Sitting there, tucked into the back was a wooden cigar box — about six inches long, five inches wide, and four inches deep. All the labels had been torn off. Remnants of ripped paper were glued to the wooden box, but it had no other discernible features as far as he could tell.

Slider reached in, grabbed the box, and pulled it out. He cautiously turned it over in his hands.

"It's just a box . . ."

"Well, that's not very exciting," she frowned.

He pondered its origin as he looked at it, but suddenly it was gone, ripped from his hands. A pair of yellow talons dug into the wood and launched into the air again.

Juliet couldn't believe her eyes. The raven flew over the rink, their box in its clutches.

"Oh, no you don't!" she said as she reached down onto one of the benches, took a hockey puck from the leftover equipment and launched it into the air.

Her aim was straight and true. The puck sailed into the sky and nailed the bird in the tail feathers. It squawked in shock, and released the box. The small wooden container plummeted to the rink below, landing right at center ice.

"Nice shot!" Slider smirked.

"I'm sporty," Juliet said. "Let's go!"

As they ran toward the rink, the outside door opened and sunlight streamed in, pouring across their faces. It caused them to stop in their tracks.

Standing in the doorway were Rodney, Buzzer, and Twitch.

"Yikes. Who are the emo triplets?" Juliet asked as the three kids walked out onto the ice. "Oh, let me guess —"

"Yep. That's them," Slider answered.

Pointing a finger in the air, Rodney let out a yell.

"Man! You smashed up my truck! You're gonna pay!"

"No, I ducked your truck and you crashed it!" Slider shot back.

"He tried to run you over?" Juliet asked.

Nodding, Slider raised his eyebrows. "Yeah."

"That's my boyfriend, jerk!" Juliet yelled back at Rodney.

Slider shot her a look of surprise. "Your wha — what?"

Shyly, she looked over at him, a bit embarrassed at her emotional outburst.

"Well, you know, you're my — my friend, and well, you are technically a boy," Juliet stammered.

Rodney rolled his eyes and looked to his goons.

"Get the box," he ordered.

In an instant, Buzzer and Twitch were on the rink, slipping and sliding toward center ice.

Reaching over, Juliet grabbed a pair of hockey sticks off the bench and tossed one to Slider. Eyes wide with excitement, Juliet grabbed Slider's arm and yanked him onto the ice.

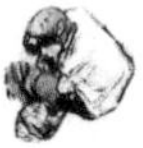

"Let's go!" she exclaimed.

"But we don't have skates!" Slider said.

"Dig the sides of your sneakers into the ice — it'll keep you from falling. Now come on!" she said, pulling him into the fray.

Rodney hung back as the raven landed on his shoulder. It looked at him and cooed as Rodney just shook his head.

"You're okay, you're okay, shhh . . ." he consoled the bird, stroking its back. Both of them observed the chaos in front of them.

On the ice, Twitch and Buzzer were closer to the box than Juliet and Slider were, but their inexperience on a frozen surface made them skid and tumble all over, giving the two friends a jump on their competition.

Buzzer jumped into the air, arms desperately reaching out for the box. At the last second, Juliet got there first and smacked it away from his grasp with an expert swipe of her stick.

"Incoming!" she yelled.

The box rocketed across the ice toward Slider. He held out his hands.

Seeing that Slider about to snatch it up, Twitch pulled the mini bat from his jacket-holster and chucked it through the air.

"Ow!" Slider yelled as the bat hit his hands, distracting him just long enough for the box to glide past him.

Bouncing off the boards, the box went wide and ricocheted back toward Twitch!

Righting himself, Slider dug his shoes in and charged at Twitch. He lifted his shoulder in the air and smashed Twitch in the side, slamming him into the boards.

He turned and ran after the box as Twitch tried to stand. The ice under the tough was so slippery, every time he tried to rise, his feet would slide out from underneath him, causing him to fall. Juliet laughed as she skated right by him.

The girl moved quickly on the sides of her sneakers, digging into the ice. As Buzzer reached for the box, her stick slapped the box with a resounding crack and once more it was knocked away from his grasp.

"Girl, you are tryin' my —" but Buzzer didn't have a chance to finish as Juliet whacked him over the head with her stick.

"That's a penalty, girlie!" Rodney's voice echoed as he suddenly came up behind Juliet and wrapped his arms around her shoulders, holding her tightly.

The box slid to a stop right at Slider's feet.

Slider bent over to pick up the box. As he got his hands near it, the box crackled with blue electricity! Slider felt a sudden burst of current go through him. It super-charged his muscles and he immediately felt energized, like he could take on the world.

And none of this got past Rodney.

He growled. Juliet struggled in his arms, trying desperately to free herself.

"No!" he yelled at Slider. "That's not for you!"

"Let her go!" Slider ordered. His voice was stronger, more authoritative.

"Don't think you can order me around, kid!" Rodney shot back. He slowly moved toward the side board's open door and path off the ice. Buzzer and Twitch limped toward him slowly.

"She's gonna be sorry if you don't hand over the box right now!" Rodney shook Juliet hard in his hands.

Eyes wide with concern, Slider placed a hand in the air and stretched out his arm. The box arced with blue electricity toward his hand.

"Here! Just — don't hurt her, please!" he pleaded as he moved toward them.

Finally off the ice, Rodney and his boys were on solid ground.

"Put it down and step back!" Rodney ordered.

But as Slider bent over to place the box on the ground, the sound of NYPD squad cars and sirens filled the air, squealing tires ripping on the pavement outside.

Slider looked over at Rodney, who clasped his hand around Juliet's mouth.

"Tonight, 11 o'clock, the skate park! Be there with the box or she will be sorry!" Rodney commanded as he and the other boys slunk into the shadows.

And as quickly as they appeared, they were gone, disappearing through the side exit as the front door suddenly blew open.

Crashing into the room, Detective Case and five uniformed officers rushed into the rink, guns drawn.

"Freeze! Police! Nobody —"

He looked around, but the only person there was Slider. Standing alone in the middle of the rink, the small wooden cigar box clutched in his hands.

"— move?" He was confused. He holstered his gun and walked toward Slider.

"They're gone already," Slider said angrily as he ran over to Case and shoved him. "They've got Juliet and you blew it!"

One after another, Slider's fists landed on Case's chest. Slider just wailed away at the detective, who stood there and took it.

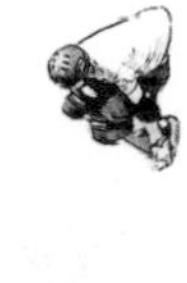

And that was it, he just couldn't help it anymore. Slider started to cry. Tears of anger, frustration, and loss flowed from his eyes as he hit Case again and again in the chest, letting out his frustrations on the cop.

"They took her! They took her!" Slider yelled, pounding on Case's chest.

Case grabbed the boy and pulled him in close, hugging him, shielding him from the other cops who looked on, completely unaware of what was happening.

"Come on, kid, let's go."

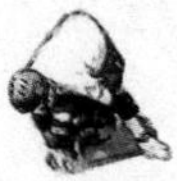

SLIDE
JULIE
NEW YORK CITY
MIKEY ADOPTED
KEY TRUST
PAVEMENT NYPD
DECK DYLAN OMA
DETECTIVE CAS
BLACK HAWK A
ENERGY ARTIFAC

9

"I told you to call me if you found anything!" Case yelled as they walked over to the car. "And that?!"

He turned and pointed at the bulge in Slider's jacket. The teen had the box tucked away for safekeeping.

"That counts as something," said the detective.

Behind him a step, Slider followed, wiping his tears away. His anger quickly returned.

"Yeah, well, who told you to come bustin' in like a tornado — siren blasting and tires screeching?" Slider fired back.

Spinning on his heels, Case got in Slider's face. He pointed a finger at his nose, about to unload on him. "Yeah! Well —" he started.

Then Case paused. He looked at the ground, thought about the situation, and relaxed.

"Okay, you're right. That was dumb," he confessed.

"And now Juliet's in trouble and there's nothing we can do!" Slider said.

Throwing open the car door, Case pointed inside. "Get in," he ordered.

Slider stopped and leaned on his skateboard.

"I'm serious. Get in," Case replied.

Frowning, Slider got in the passenger side. He slammed the door so hard that the glass shook.

Case stopped and watched as the car rocked back and forth a bit. "Wow," he said, surprised at Slider's strength. "That was impressive."

Getting in the driver's side, Case slammed the door himself, but it was nowhere near as hard as Slider had done. His eyes grew narrow and a thin smile passed over his lips. He knew what that meant.

"Give me the box, kid," Case said as he reached out his hand.

"I don't know —" Slider began.

"Now!" commanded Case.

The teen paused a beat, but Slider finally reached into his jacket. He pulled out the small, wooden box, cradling it in his hands.

"Wait. Did you open it?" Case asked as he looked down at the cigar box.

"No."

"Do it," Case ordered the boy.

"What? No, I —" Slider was baffled and shocked at the detective's order, but Case didn't back down.

Slowly, Slider unlatched the small, brass clasp and pressed it up. Thumb on the lid, Slider pulled up slightly, opening the box and peeking inside.

What he saw didn't impress him at all.

"That's it?!" he exclaimed. "That's what all this fighting's been about?"

Nestled inside the wooden container, on top of several strips of newspaper insulation, sat the broken tail of an old skateboard. Splintered and frayed, the wooden kicktail still had part of its grip tape intact on top. However, the graphic on the bottom was almost scraped off from overuse. The Artifact measured three inches wide and six inches long.

"A broken skateboard deck! Really? Seriously? This is so stupid!" Slider pulled the Artifact out of the box and waved it in the air, upset and confused.

Case gazed at Slider's hand gripping the board piece and shaking it violently.

"Kid, look — look at your hand!" he said.

Slider's face suddenly changed from anger to shock at what he saw.

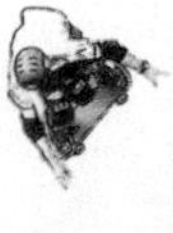

A stream of electricity flowed over his hand. The strange energy enveloped it, making a slight crackling sound. It trickled out of the board and onto Slider's fingers and palm.

"What is this?" asked Slider.

The teen started to get scared. He'd never seen anything or heard of anything like this before. The blue bolts leaped from fingertip to fingertip as he wiggled the broken board in his hands.

Smiling from ear to ear, Case tried to calm him.

"Kid, that's the Artifact!" he explained.

"What?" Slider squeaked out.

"It likes you," said the detective. "I don't know why, but man does it like you!"

"That's great," said Slider. "But what is it?"

Case shook his head and shrugged. "Seriously, we don't really know. I mean that? That's a kicktail from a broken skateboard. But the energy —? Some people think it's a key. One that, when assembled with all its other parts, will unlock some kind of power . . . . If those guys were to get their hands on it, who knows where it could end up. We can't let that happen!"

Quickly, Slider placed the tailfin back in the box. He slammed the lid, locking the latch back in place.

The electricity promptly stopped.

"I don't care," he said and quickly handed the box to Detective Case.

"What do you mean you don't care?" Case was irritated, but Slider wouldn't hear it.

"They've got Juliet, and they want that!" Slider pointed at the box. "I just want her back, man. I don't care about this thing at all! But I *do* care about her!"

"I thought the only person you cared about was yourself?" The detective smirked as he looked Slider dead in the eyes.

"Well, things change, man," he said softly.

"Sorry kid, they can't get their hands on this," the detective said sternly.

"But they're gonna hurt her!" Slider pleaded.

Case stared off into space for a moment. Then he turned back to Slider and smiled.

He looked down at the skateboard in Slider's lap and laughed. "Maybe not . . ."

* * *

Late that night, Rodney, Buzzer, Twitch, and Juliet arrived at the skate park. Buzzer and Twitch leaped from the back truck bed and landed on the ground.

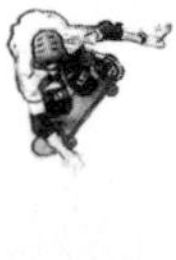

Juliet sat in the front seat. Her feet and wrists were bound with duct tape, and her mouth had been gagged with a handkerchief.

Rodney turned to Juliet and smiled. "Now don't move," he said quietly. From under the dashboard, the teen pulled the parking brake on. "We'll be done in a minute. If your boyfriend actually does what we tell him, you'll be home in no time."

Juliet struggled a bit. Rodney just laughed as he turned to open the truck door.

But the door was stuck shut.

The earlier impact that night had crumpled the front engine compartment and the side panel. Opening either door was nearly impossible.

Juliet chuckled through the handkerchief as Rodney slammed his shoulder against the door, again and again.

"Come over here and help!" he yelled at his companions. But as they walked over, the door popped. Rodney hit Buzzer and Twitch with the door, sending them flying to the ground, tumbling over one another.

"Get up! You're embarrassing me!" Rodney said, striding past them.

On the other side of the park, Slider stood with one foot on his board and backpack over his arm. He glanced over his shoulder into the darkness, skeptical of himself.

A sudden flash of light from Case's high beams signaled the detective's readiness.

"This had better work!" Slider whispered into his jacket collar.

Tucked away, on the underside of his lapel, a small transmitting device sat undetected. In his ear, a miniature receiver linked the teen to the detective.

"It will, kid," the detective radioed back. "Trust me. And don't worry. Backup's on the way."

Slider kicked off down the path toward the skate park.

Meanwhile, inside the car, the detective sat holding a small headphone cup to his ear. He could hear Slider's wheels grind on the pavement.

"Great, more cops," Slider said into the his collar.

Case smiled and shook his head. "No, something a little different," he started to explain.

"Whatever. Just do your part, okay?" said Slider.

Entering the gate, Rodney strained his eyes in the darkness, looking for Slider. He didn't see the skater anywhere as he and the other two boys moved to the center of the park.

"Where is he?" Rodney yelled.

The teen turned his head toward the raven on his shoulder. "Find him," Rodney whispered to the bird.

The bird launched high into the air, dipping in and out of lamplight and the darkness. A squawk echoed as the bird turned tail and flew back toward the trio.

"Where?" Rodney said to the raven as it landed on his shoulder.

"Here!" a voice called out from behind them.

The teens spun to see Slider enter the skate park with his bag over his shoulder. He was about thirty yards away, half in and half out of the light cascading down from above.

"That's far enough," yelled Rodney.

Slider looked around, but didn't see Juliet.

"Where is she?" he asked loudly.

"Do you have what I want?" Rodney asked.

Slider removed the bag from his shoulder and waved it high in the air. "It's here! Now where's Juliet?" he asked with concern.

"Oh yes, Juliet — sweet Juliet," Rodney said as he moved toward Slider.

In the car, Case was getting impatient. "Come on, Slider, spill it! Where is she?" the detective mumbled as he listened in through the headset. "You've got to make him tell you where she is!"

"Where?" Slider demanded again. "If you want the Artifact, you'll tell me!"

Rodney nodded toward his truck. "In the cab of my truck," he said.

"Gotcha! I'm going off communications," radioed the detective. "You're on your own, Slider!"

Case bolted from his car and started toward the skate park. Moving stealthily through the dark, Case found the truck. It sat 100 yards ahead of him, parked at the top of the hill leading past the skate park. The outline of the crumpled hood caught the reflection of the moonlight. He was seconds away from the door.

Inside the truck cab, Juliet squirmed and struggled to get free. Twisting and turning her wrists, she tried to break the tape that held her hands together. It was too strong.

Juliet repeatedly kicked out at the door, trying to get it open. She could try to worm her way out and try to crawl away. Unfortunately, the door was still too damaged to even unlatch.

However, each time she kicked the door, the parking brake slipped a little more. With each of her forceful footfalls, the brake was slowly coming loose.

Case reached the back of the truck. Suddenly, the parking brake sprung off with a loud click. The truck began creeping forward, rolling away. It moved slowly at first, but then started picking up speed.

Case stopped, stood up straight, and scratched his head. The truck was slipping away from him.

When Juliet popped her head up in the back window, Case gave chase.

* * *

"Give me the box," Rodney shouted, putting out a waiting hand.

Slider flung the bag at him.

Rodney caught it and eagerly ripped the zipper open. "Come on —!" he mumbled, digging around the bag.

Finally, a smile crossed his lips. Rodney pulled the box from the bag. Opening it, the teen saw the broken piece of skateboard inside. He nodded toward the truck.

"Smart boy," said Rodney. "Go, let her out!"

The boys turned and stopped dead in their tracks. Slider and all of the goons watched as the truck rolled down the hill, the cop chasing after it like a madman.

Shooting a look at Rodney, Slider's eyes were crazy-mad, but Rodney just shrugged. "Don't look at me, pal. I put the brake on!"

"Stupid grown-ups," Slider sighed. He took off on his board.

Buzzer and Twitch looked after Slider and nodded to Rodney.

"Shouldn't we go after him?" Buzzer asked.

"Why?" said Rodney. "We have the Artifact and that truck's all beat up anyway —"

Rodney looked up and saw Slider pick up speed. When he got to the end of the block, Slider stopped and picked up his skateboard off the ground. A strange electrical energy began to surround the boy. His skin hissed and crackled with power.

"How's he doing that?" shouted Buzzer, shielding his eyes against the glow.

Rodney focused on Slider's deck as he passed under a street lamp.

The tail of Slider's board had been broken off.

"Son of a —!" Rodney yelled.

He ripped open the box and grabbed the Artifact. No electricity came from the piece at all. This piece was the broken kicktail off Slider's own board. They'd been tricked!

"It's a fake!" shouted Rodney. "Get him!"

WELCOME TO THE REVOLUTION SLIDER

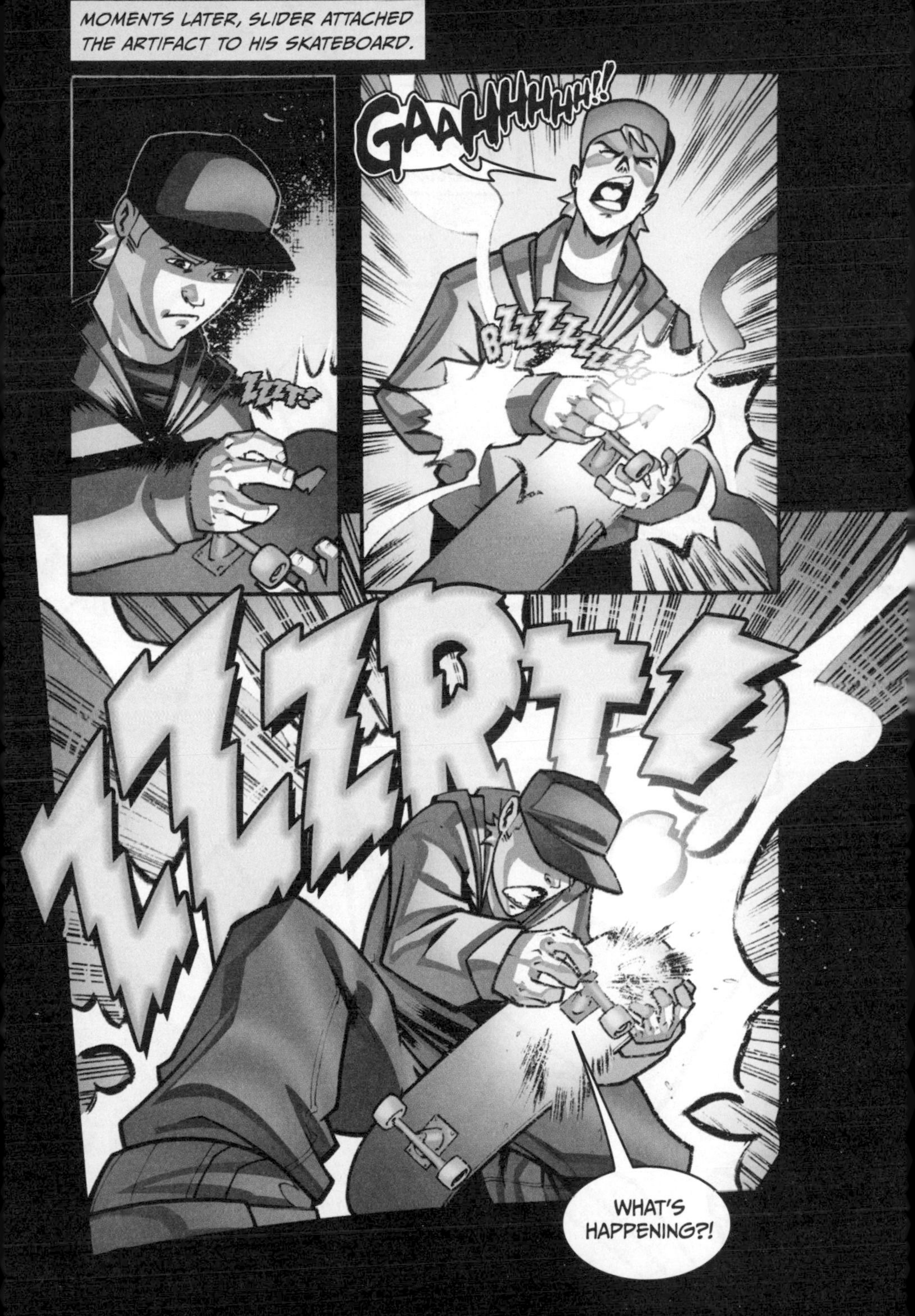
MOMENTS LATER, SLIDER ATTACHED THE ARTIFACT TO HIS SKATEBOARD.
ZZZT!
GAAHHHHHH!!
BZZZZZZZT!
ZZZRT!
WHAT'S HAPPENING?!

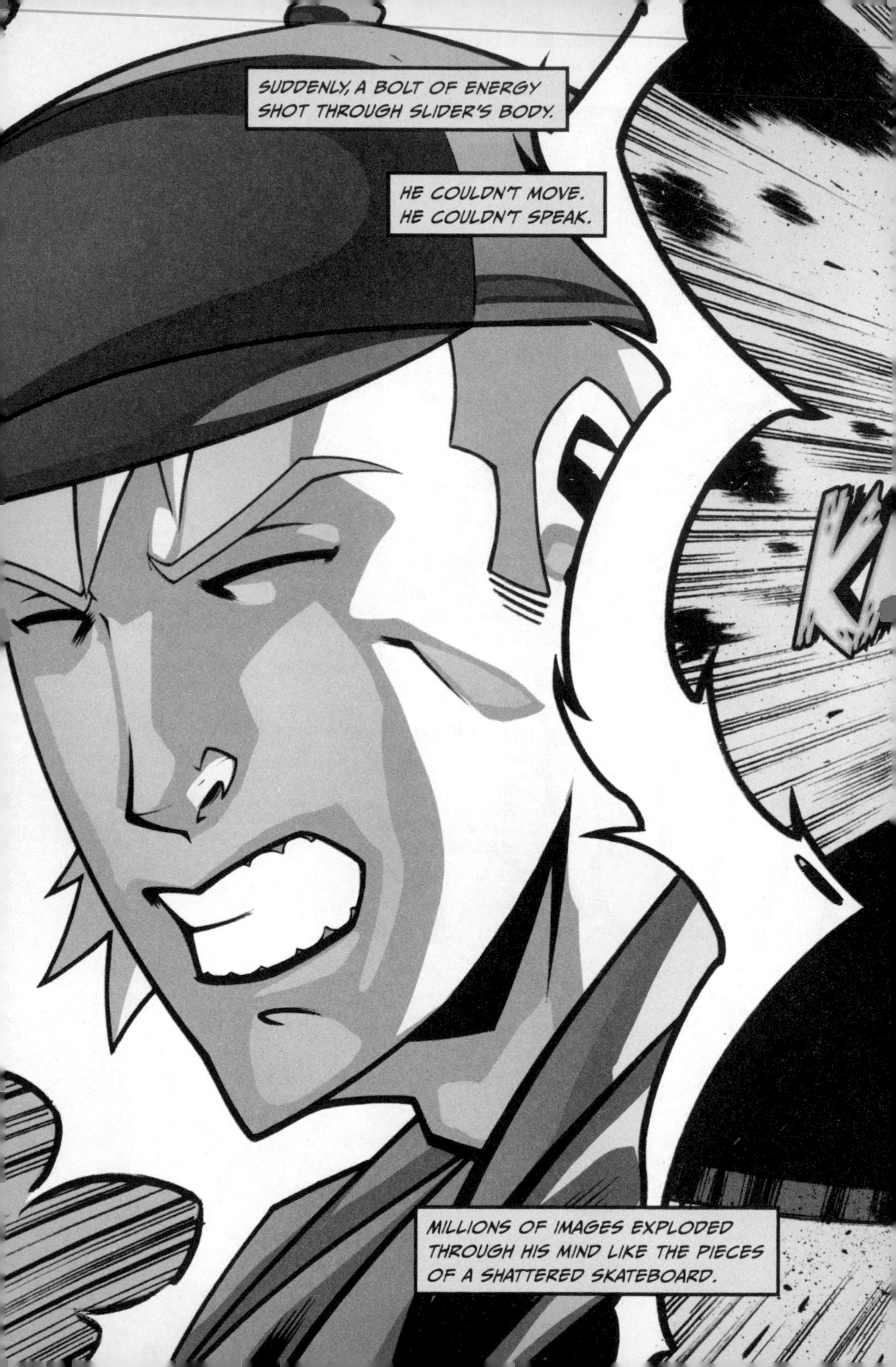
SUDDENLY, A BOLT OF ENERGY SHOT THROUGH SLIDER'S BODY.
HE COULDN'T MOVE. HE COULDN'T SPEAK.
MILLIONS OF IMAGES EXPLODED THROUGH HIS MIND LIKE THE PIECES OF A SHATTERED SKATEBOARD.

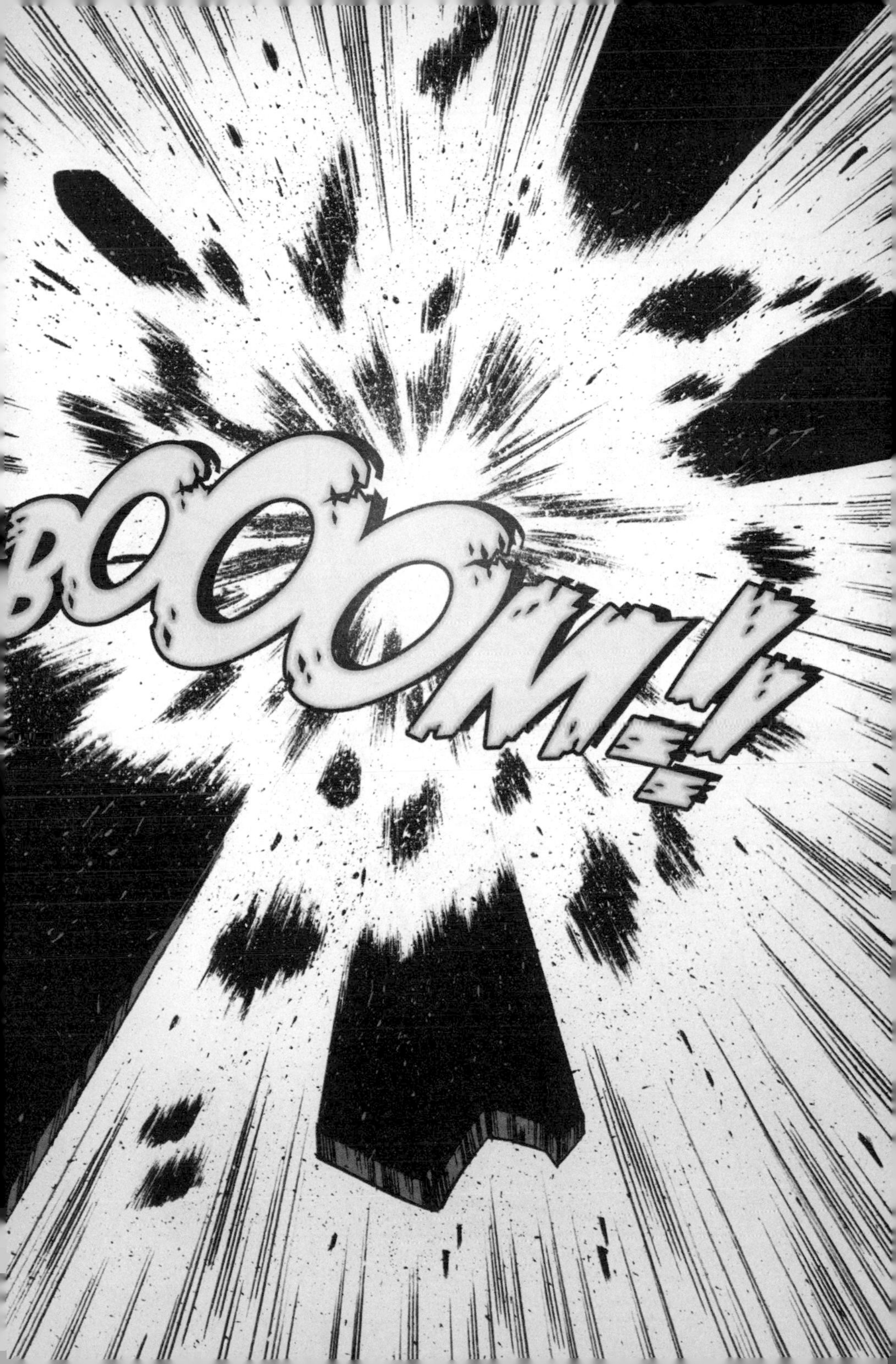
BOOOM!!

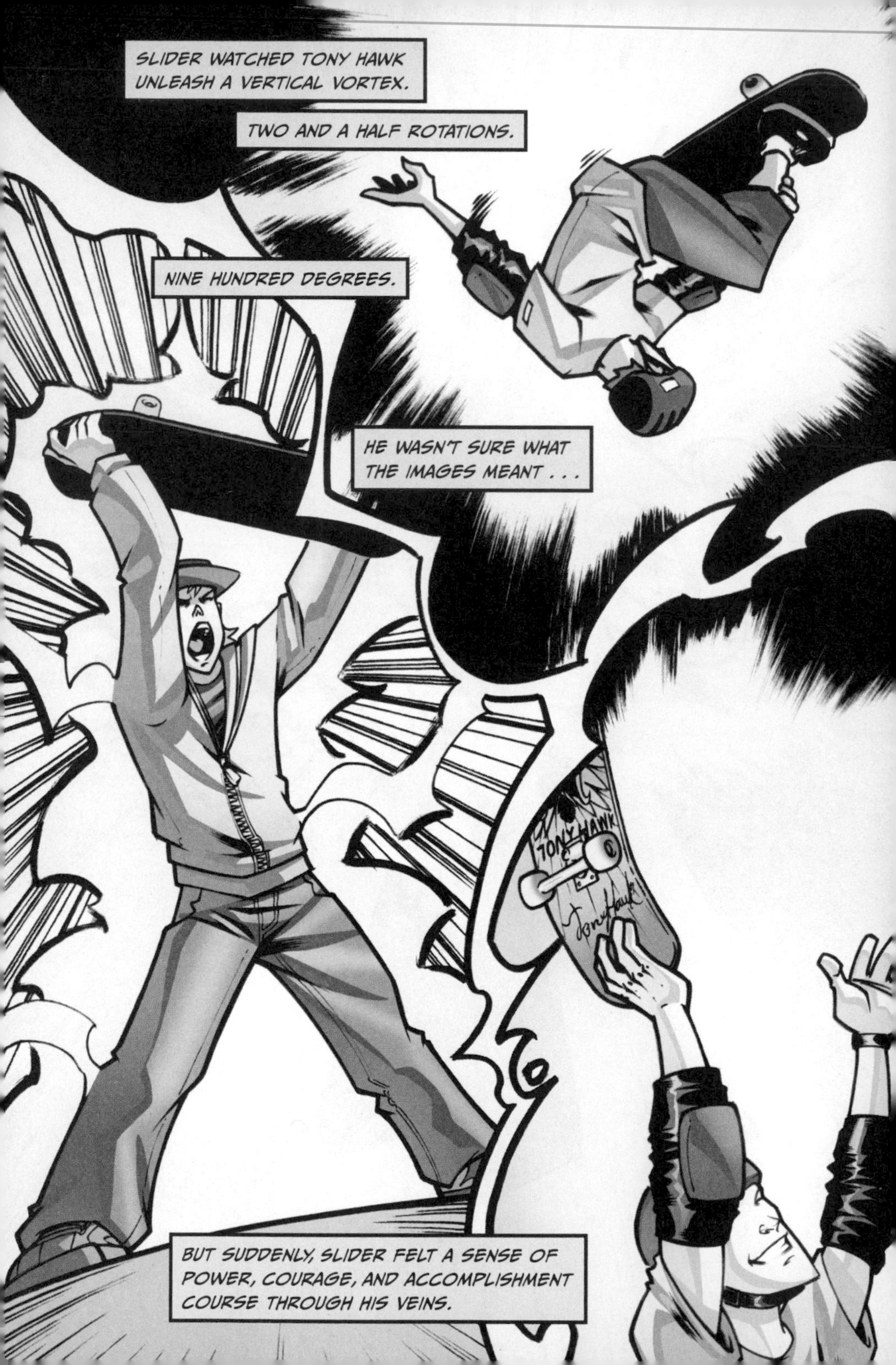
SLIDER WATCHED TONY HAWK UNLEASH A VERTICAL VORTEX.
TWO AND A HALF ROTATIONS.
NINE HUNDRED DEGREES.
HE WASN'T SURE WHAT THE IMAGES MEANT . . .
TONY HAWK
BUT SUDDENLY, SLIDER FELT A SENSE OF POWER, COURAGE, AND ACCOMPLISHMENT COURSE THROUGH HIS VEINS.

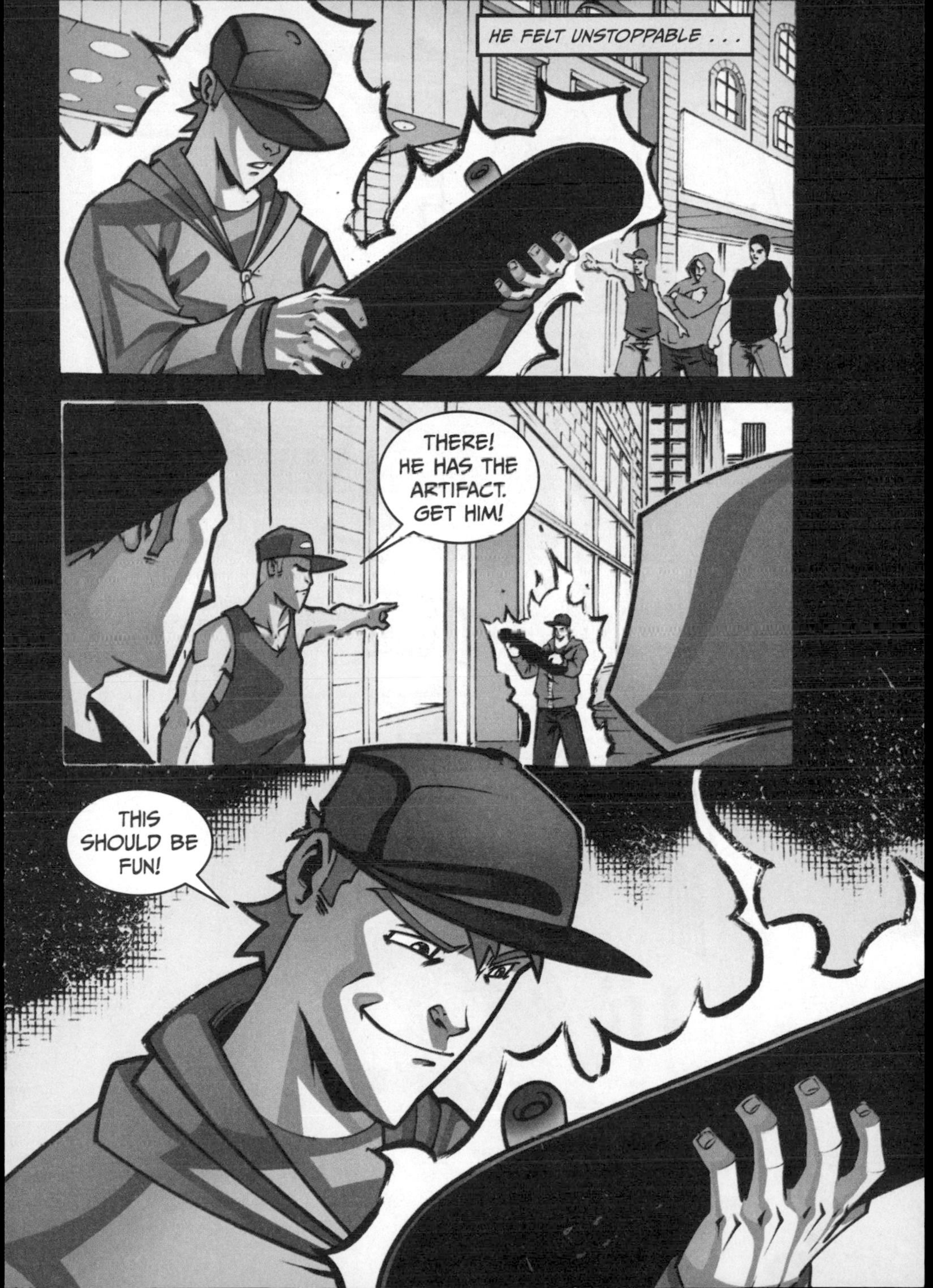
HE FELT UNSTOPPABLE . . .
THERE! HE HAS THE ARTIFACT. GET HIM!
THIS SHOULD BE FUN!

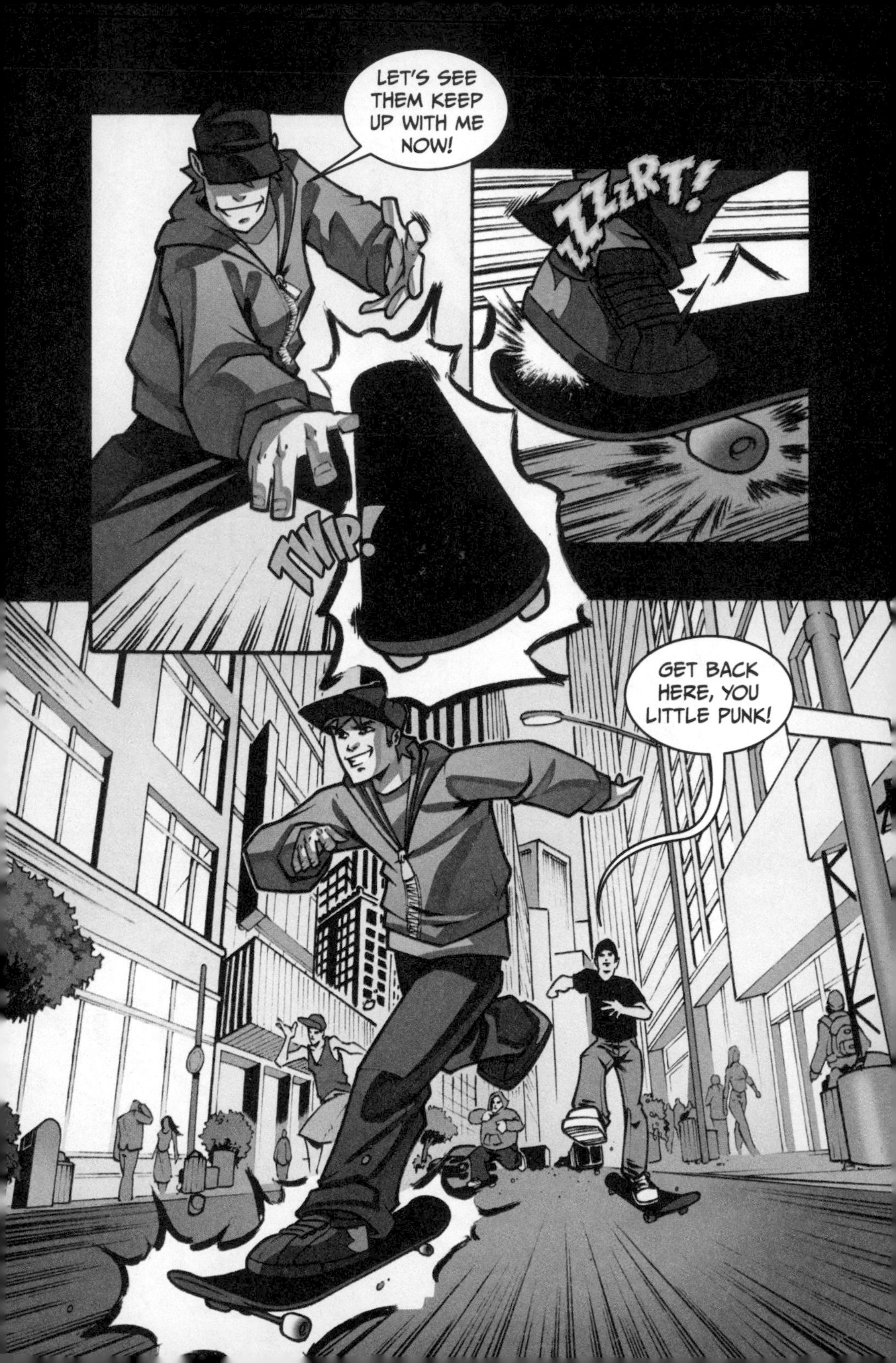
LET'S SEE THEM KEEP UP WITH ME NOW!
ZZZzRT!
TWIP!
GET BACK HERE, YOU LITTLE PUNK!

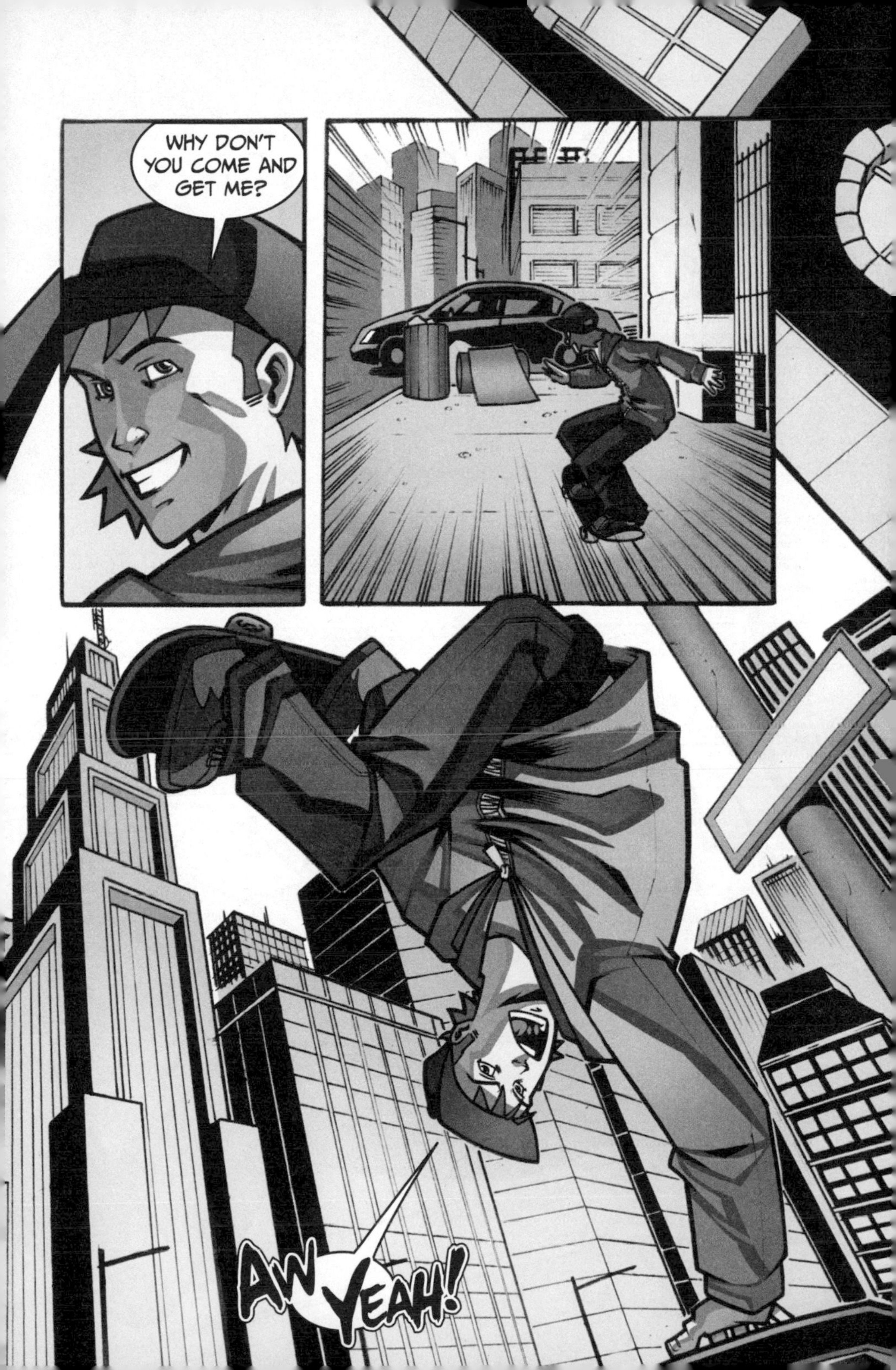
WHY DON'T YOU COME AND GET ME?
AW YEAH!

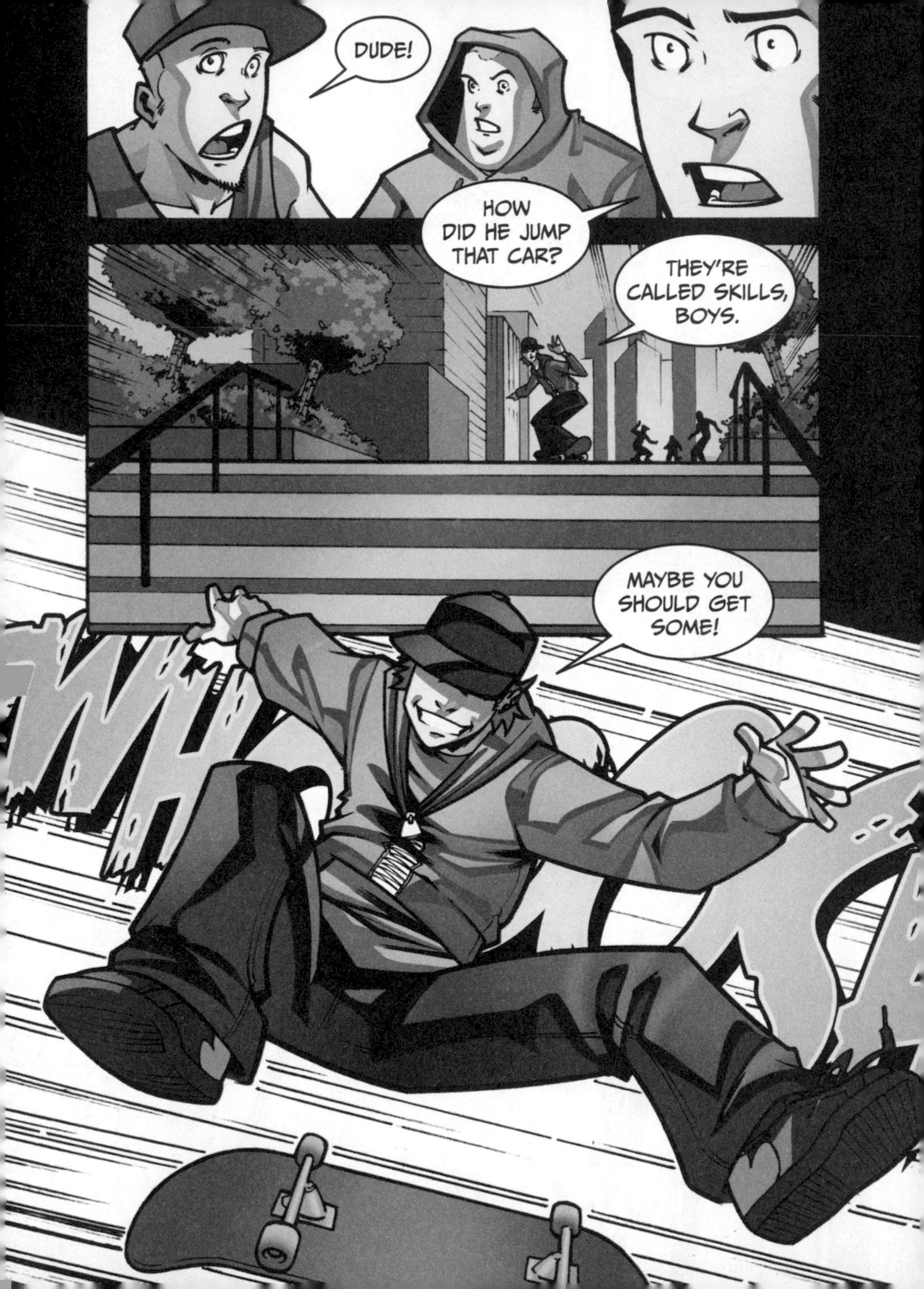
DUDE!
HOW DID HE JUMP THAT CAR?
THEY'RE CALLED SKILLS, BOYS.
MAYBE YOU SHOULD GET SOME!

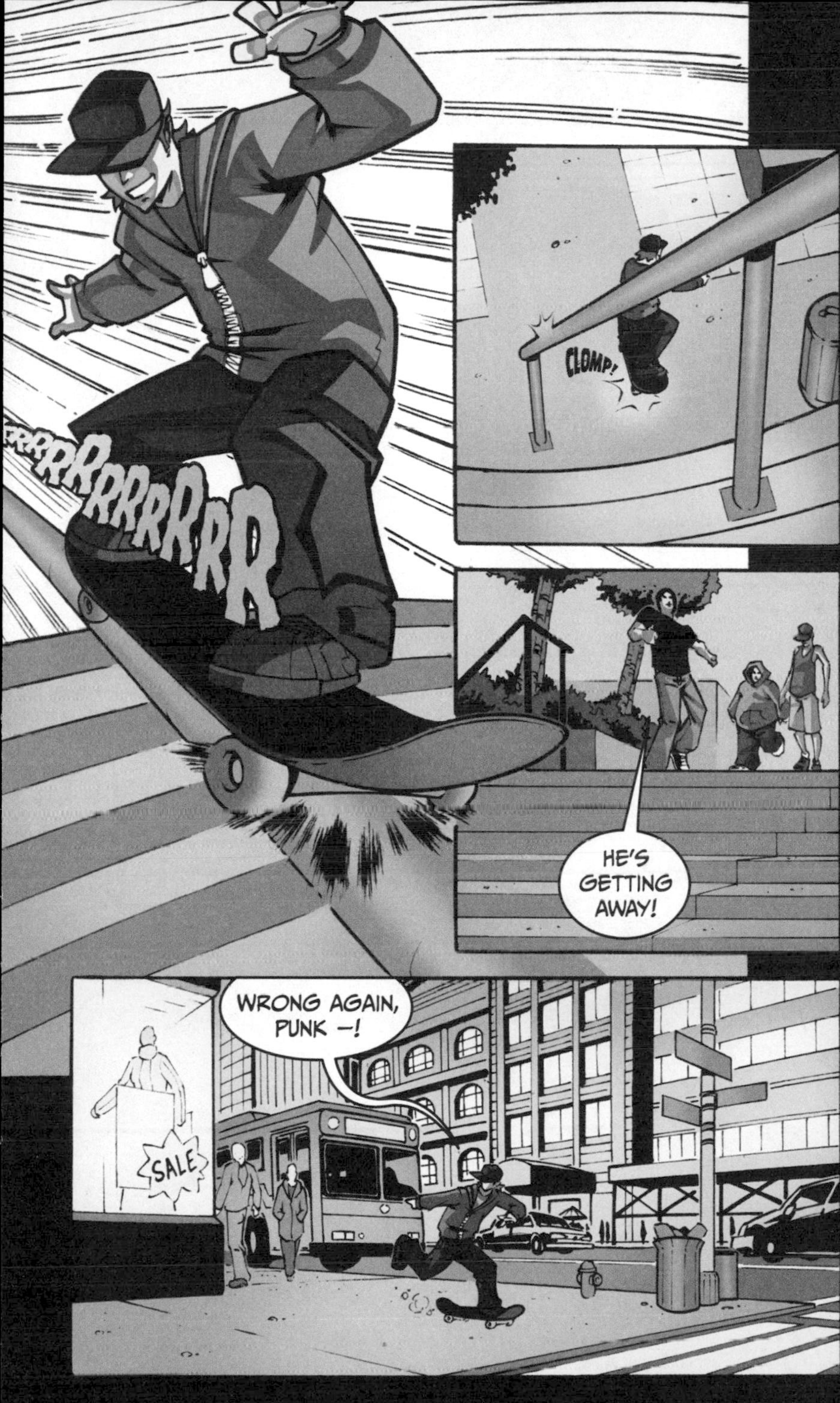
RRRRRRRRRRRRR
CLOMP!
HE'S GETTING AWAY!
WRONG AGAIN, PUNK --!
SALE

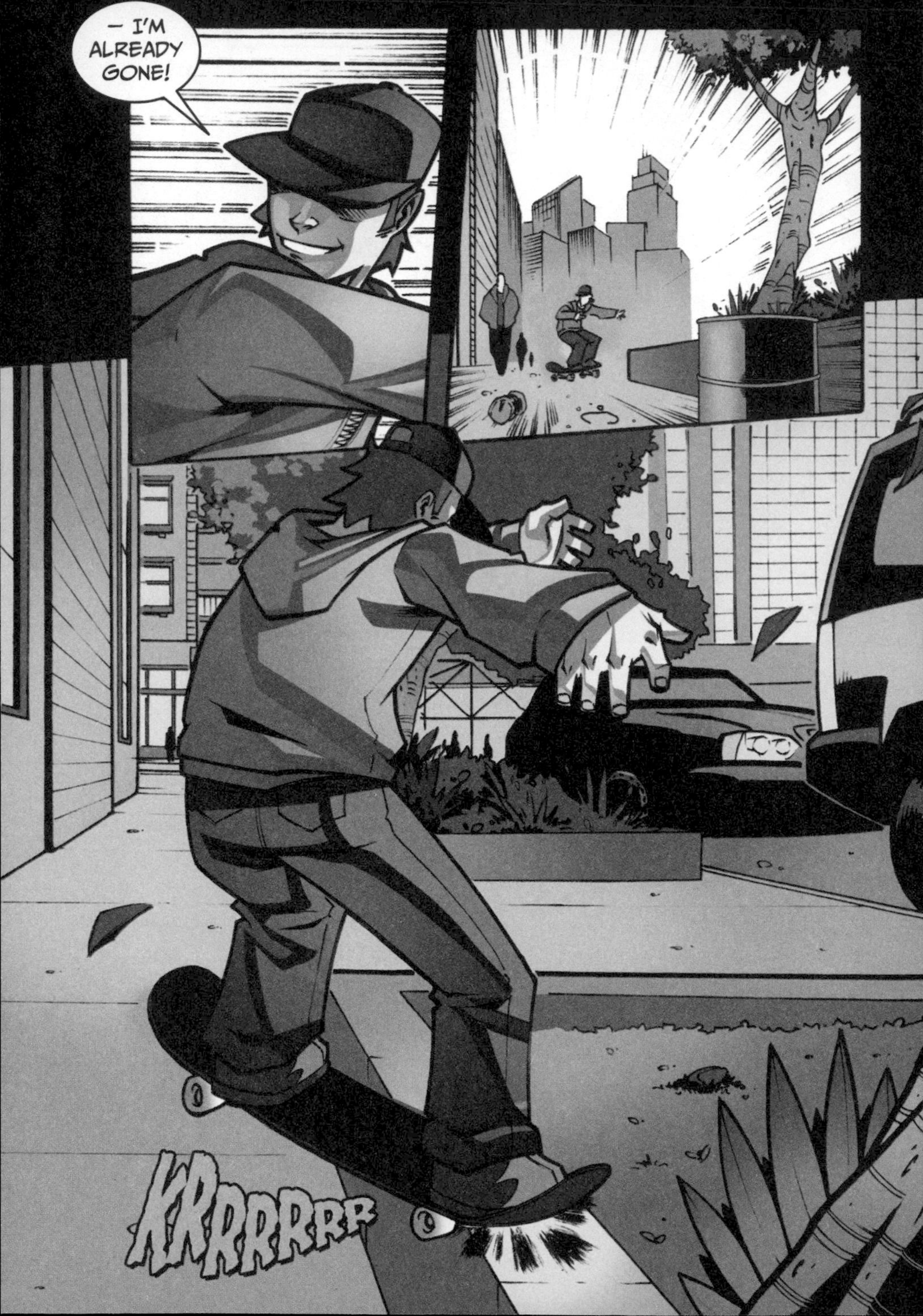
– I'M ALREADY GONE!
KRRRRRR

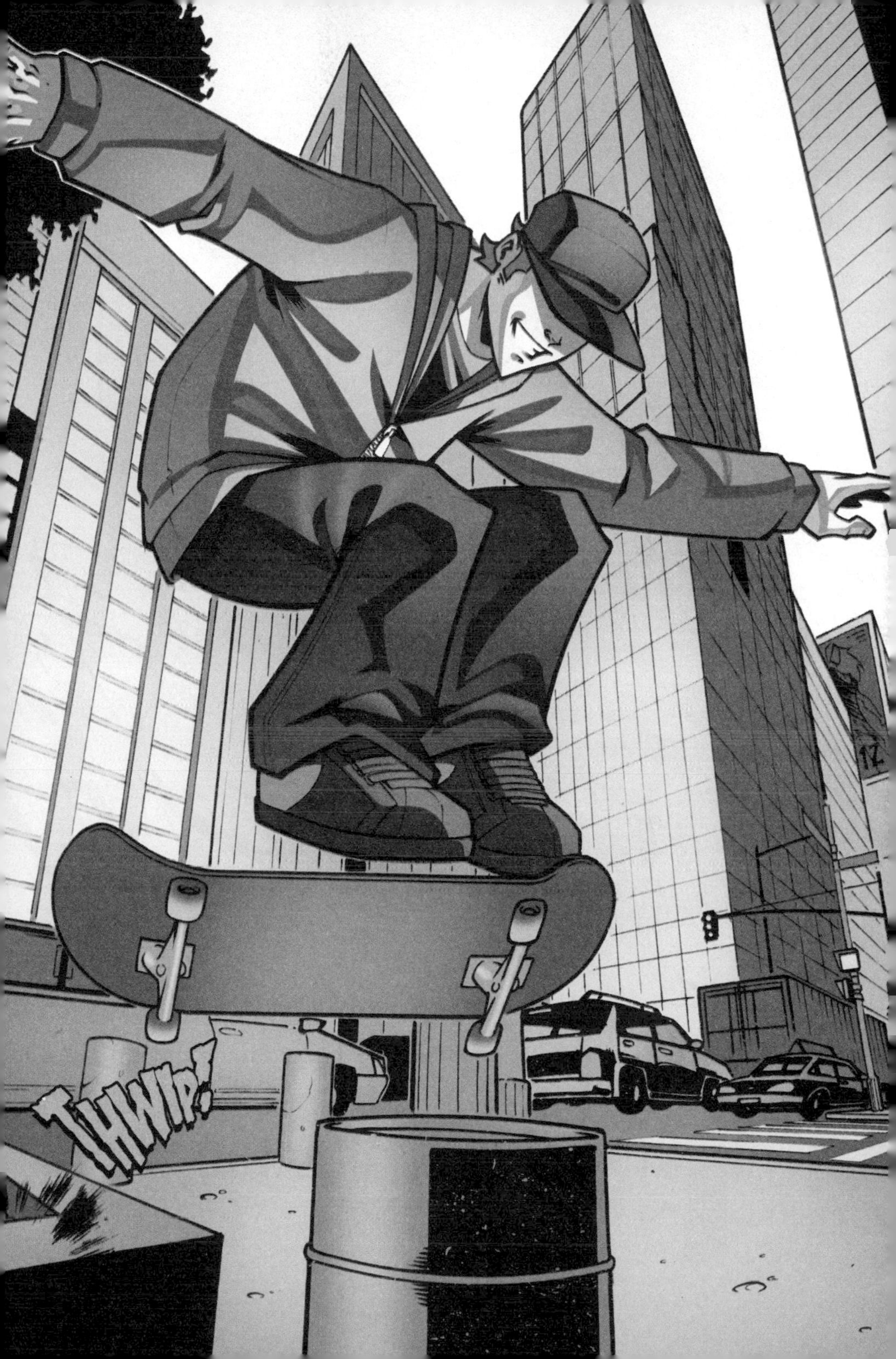
THWIP!

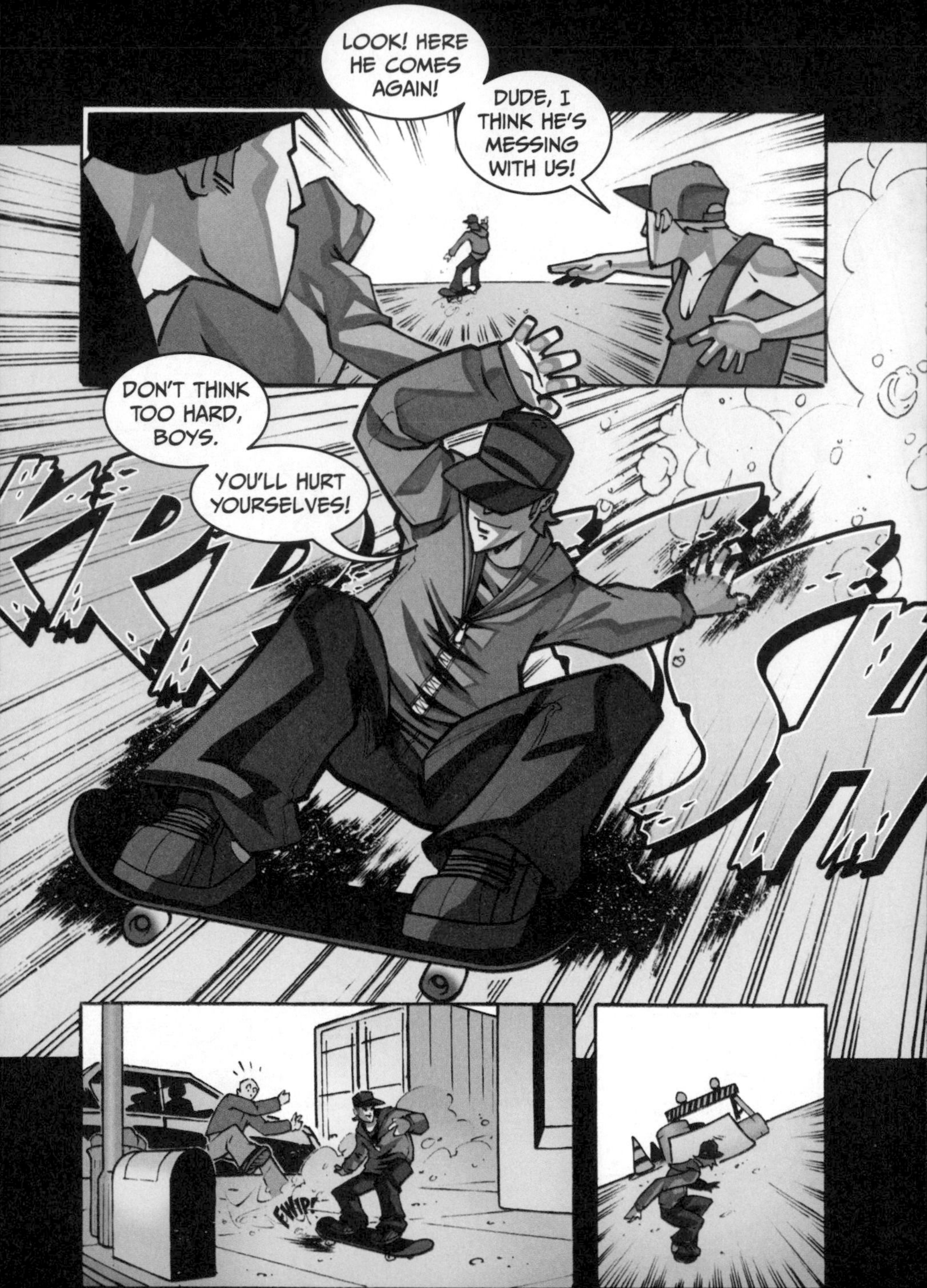
LOOK! HERE HE COMES AGAIN!
DUDE, I THINK HE'S MESSING WITH US!
DON'T THINK TOO HARD, BOYS.
YOU'LL HURT YOURSELVES!
EWIP!

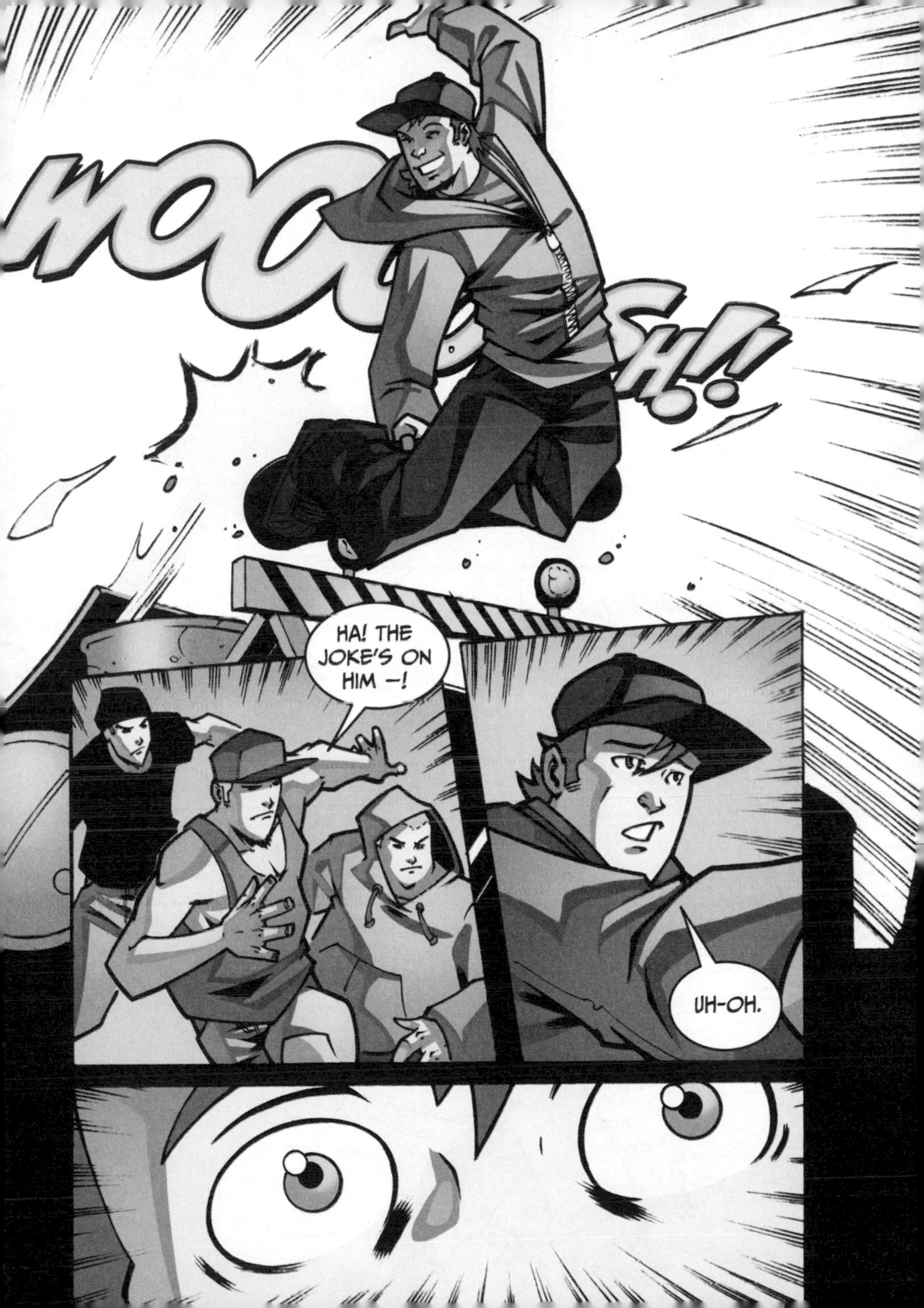
WOOOSH!!
HA! THE JOKE'S ON HIM –!
UH-OH.

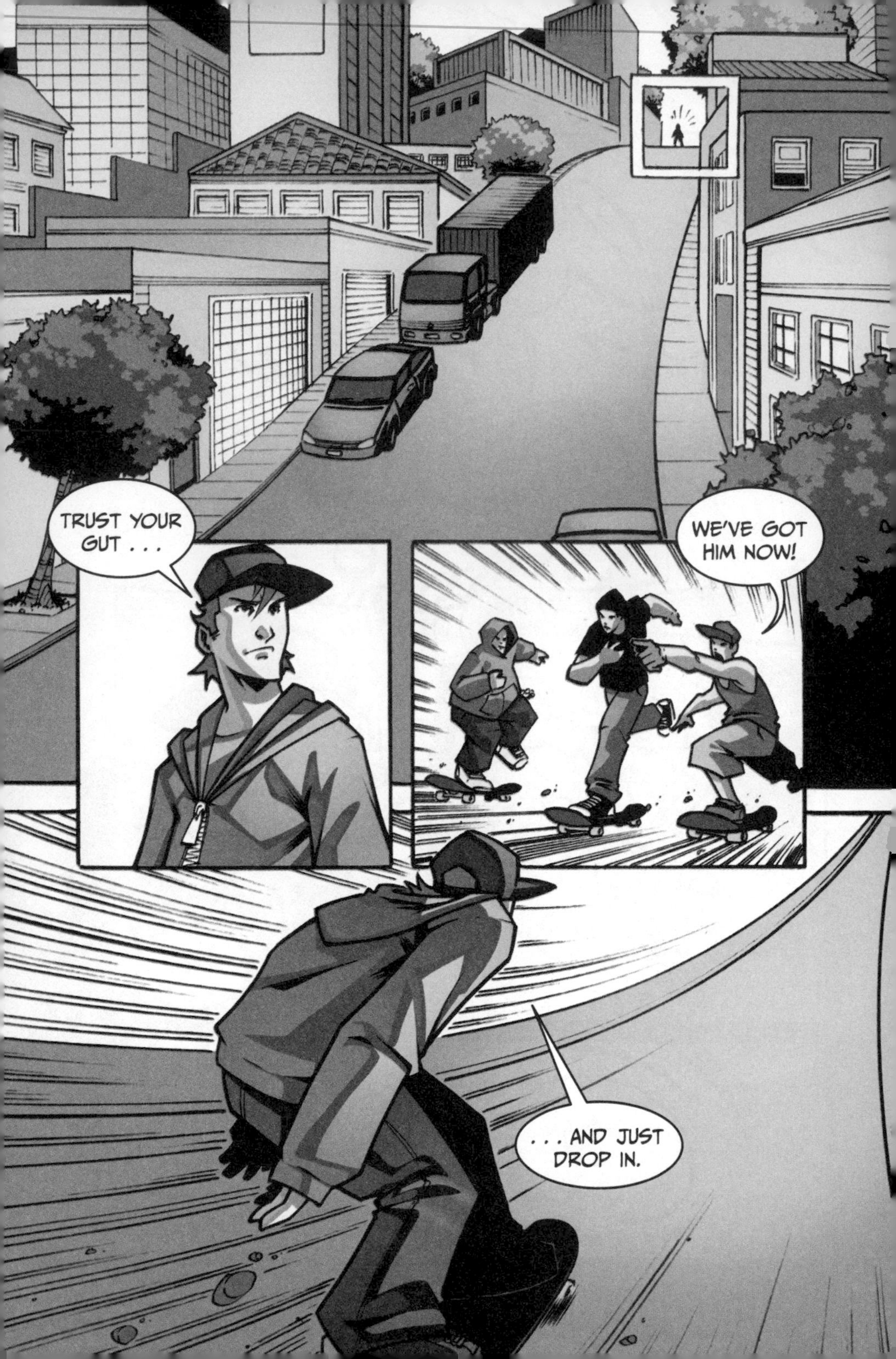
TRUST YOUR GUT . . .
WE'VE GOT HIM NOW!
. . . AND JUST DROP IN.

TONY HAWK'S 900 revolution

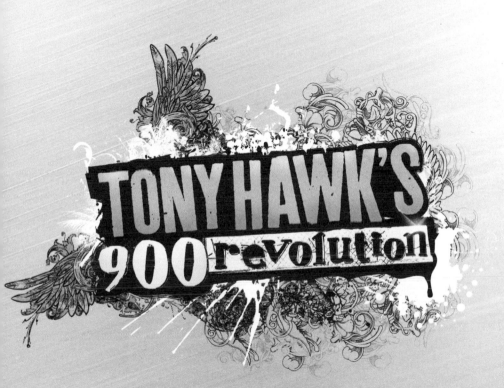

R MIKES HAUNTED
KEY TRUST
MOVEMENT HYP
DECK DYLAN OMA
DETECTIVE CAS
D BLACK HAWK A
ENERGY ARTIFAC

10

On the sidewalks, Buzzer and Twitch continued chasing Slider. This time, however, Rodney was close behind — and gaining.

Kicking with all his might, Slider turned left, sailed down a hill, and entered a walkway surrounded by trees.

Buzzer followed first, as he was the closest to Slider's tail.

Reaching the other end of the walkway, Slider stopped and reached up. He clutched onto a tree branch and pulled it backward.

Buzzer closed in, but got a tree in the face as Slider let go of the branch. "Ah!" Buzzer yelled as he flew backward off his board. He rolled on the ground, smacking his head on the pavement and knocking himself unconscious.

Picking up his board, Slider headed up the side of a small hill and back onto the main road.

But over his head as he climbed, Twitch launched over him with a heel flip. He popped Slider in the head with his board.

"Whoa!" Slider yelled out loud as he ducked.

His cap absorbed the impact and shifted forward, covering his eyes. Slider pushed it back in time to see Twitch land perfectly and grind to a stop.

"Lucky you've got a cap on, punk, or I'd have taken your head off!" Twitch turned and scowled as Slider took off.

*　*　*

Meanwhile, Case continued after the truck. He poured on the speed and finally got parallel to the driver's door. Inside, Juliet looked out at him with fear.

"Don't worry," Case huffed. "We'll —"

Juliet turned and looked out ahead. Suddenly, the girl's eyes went wide. She whipped back toward Case and tried to scream, but her gagged mouth muffled the words.

"No! Don't panic! I'll get you out!" said the detective.

Juliet shook her head and nodded toward the front of the truck, finally getting him to look forward.

"What are you looking —?"

As Case turned, he got a faceful of Douglas Fir pine tree. The detective was flat on his back, and the truck kept rolling along.

"Ohhhh. So that's what you're looking at . . . !" the detective moaned.

*   *   *

Moving through the park, his wheels burning up the pavement, Slider soared down a ramp and leaned right. He entered a large drainage tunnel.

Then he noticed Twitch on the far end. He stood about 50 yards away, blocking the exit.

Knowing better, Slider turned back the way he'd come in. But he didn't stop. Rodney was skating up fast behind him.

He was trapped.

Quickly, Slider looked at his surroundings and weighed his options.

Picking up a tree limb, the teen eyed Twitch and started kicking, heading right for him!

Twitch smiled and yelled. "Chicken? I never lose to you, punk!"

Twitch reached inside his jacket and pulled out the mini baseball bat. "Let's play!"

They headed toward one another, picking up speed.

Twitch closed his hand around his bat and smiled.

"Batter up!" Twitch yelled as he raised the weapon in the air.

But as Slider moved into range, he pushed hard on the back of his deck, flipping the front wheels up. Twisting the back of the deck at a 45-degree angle, he kicked up without losing any speed. Slider shot up the side of the pipe.

In a flash, he was corkscrewing up and over his attacker. Stunned, Twitch watched as Slider skated up the side of the tunnel wall and over the top of him!

Twitch completely missed Slider tossing the large branch onto the floor of he tunnel. He placed it right in front of his attacker's board.

Coming down the other side of the pipe, Slider didn't even look back as he exited the tunnel and cut left.

Crunch! Twitch's board hit the branch. The boy was thrown from the deck and into the air. He hit the ground hard and skidded along the tunnel. When he finally came to a stop, he was unconscious.

* * *

Case couldn't catch up to the truck. It was rolling away too quickly, and he was out of gas. He stopped, grabbed his knees, and sucked in lungfuls of air.

Skating up next to him, Slider stopped as well. "What happened? Where's Juliet?" he asked the detective.

Case was so winded he could barely even talk. "Inside!" he said, pointing toward the rolling truck.

"It's heading for the lake!" Slider yelled.

Off like a shot, Slider skated down the hill.

* * *

Picking up speed, the truck rolled through the grass toward the lake. Barreling out of control, it smashed through a park bench. Shards of wooden shrapnel and metal frame shattered the truck's windshield. Bits of safety glass showered Juliet as she struggled to get free.

* * *

Unfortunately for Slider, there was no direct route that followed the exact path of the truck.

Expertly, he skated after the truck on the sidewalks. He hopped from one sidewalk to another, barely avoiding the clumps of grass in between that would send any skater flying.

Small switchbacks in the road were too tight to take as high-speed turns. Slider popped a series of ollies to get over these small hurdles.

Slider launched over them perpendicularly, and
finally he came to a path that overlooked the truck's
route perfectly.

The path turned. Slider turned with it as the
sidewalk angled closer to the truck.

Kicking harder and harder, he now matched the
speed of the truck, and could watch it from his higher
vantage point. But he couldn't get any closer.

About fifty yards away, the hillside suddenly stopped
and fell off abruptly, ending in a sheer 20-foot drop into
the lake.

He watched helplessly as the truck zoomed along,
careening toward the cliff.

A steep staircase at the end of the trail led down
to the grassy knoll the truck was rolling toward. But
even if he got there before the truck, he had no way of
stopping it. He wasn't a superhero; he couldn't grab it
or stand in front of it.

What could he do?

His mind raced for a solution as he looked from the
staircase to the truck and back again.

Going flat-out fast, he headed toward the cement
staircase. Right at the edge of the stairs, he kicked down
hard on the back of his board.

In an instant, his wheels left the pavement.

He spun in midair, bringing his legs up, and pulled the board to his feet.

Launching off the top of the staircase, Slider flipped the board over and did a reverse varial heelflip in the air, slowing his forward momentum just enough to be moving right over the truck's location. As he started his descent, the truck was right below him.

With a resounding thud of plastic wheels on sheet metal, Slider came down perfectly in the bed of the moving vehicle.

In front of them, the lake came into view.

"Hola!" he yelled through the back window as he stuck his head in the cab. Eyes wide, Juliet squirmed as he reached in and grabbed the parking break, yanking as hard as he could.

Locking up, the wheels of the truck stopped spinning, but the weight and sheer momentum of the metal beast continued to drive forward. It skidded in the grass. Then it suddenly rotated a full 180 degrees and started going backward.

Slider was thrown to the left, barely able to keep from being thrown out of the bed.

The truck chewed up dirt and turf as it ground toward the cliff's edge in reverse. Desperate and not sure what to do, Slider quickly weighed his options.

When Slider looked behind him, he saw they were thirty feet from the edge and he had only seconds to act.

Instinctively, he climbed through the rear window and into the cab.

"Hold on!" Slider yelled as he grabbed Juliet around the waist.

Holding her with all his strength, Slider climbed out onto the hood of the truck and, pressing his feet firmly, he leaped forward.

As the rear bed of the truck crashed through the guardrail and dipped over the cliff, the body of the truck began to fall.

He and Juliet sailed upward through the air. The truck dropped from their feet and disappeared over the cliff.

They landed on the edge of the grass and rolled to safety as the sound of crumpling metal and shattering glass rang out through the night. Then, a massive explosion boomed outward as the truck hit the rocks below them. Heat and light from the fireball filled the sky.

Slider jumped to his feet and rushed over to Juliet, ripping the duct tape from her face.

"Are you okay?" he asked her.

Juliet smiled at him.

"How — how did you just do that?" she asked.

"He's got the power in him now!" a voice yelled from the darkness.

R MIKEY ADOPTE

KEY TRUST

PAVEMENT NYP

DECK DYLAN OMA

DETECTIVE CAS

D BLACK HAWK A

A ENERGY ARTIFAC

11

Juliet and Slider turned and looked as Rodney emerged from behind a tree and walked toward them, holding his board.

"A power that wasn't meant for him!" he yelled as he held his board in both hands. Crackles of red electricity spewed from the board, filling Rodney's hands as it leaped from the wood to his flesh and swarmed over his hands the way the blue energy had floated over Slider's.

But this energy? Slider sensed it was evil, pure and simple, and Rodney loved it. He seemed to be pulling strength from it.

Dropping the deck to the grass, Rodney balled his hands into fists.

"I want that Artifact, and I want it now!"

"Is this what you want, Rodney?!" a voice boomed.

Turning, all three of them froze and stared.

"No!" Rodney exclaimed.

Fifty yards away stood Omar Grebes, the real Artifact in his hand. Blue electricity flowed from it, illuminating Omar's face as he held it in the air.

"Come and get it, Rodney," Omar smiled.

Rodney dropped his board to the ground and stepped on it, backpedaling. He pointed at them all as he yelled.

"Another time, Omar! And *you!*"

He pointed right at Slider.

"I'll see you again, kid! Count on that!"

His words trailed off as he skated into the darkness.

"I'll be waiting, punk!" Slider yelled after him.

Coming up behind them, Case finally arrived on the scene, out of breath.

"Man! You . . . you all . . . okay?" he asked.

Looking up at him, Slider smiled. "Are *you*, old man? You're not gonna have a heart attack, are you?"

"Funny, real funny . . ." Case bent down and ripped the duct tape from Juliet's wrists and ankles, helping her to her feet.

Slider stared at Omar, looking him up and down suspiciously. The stranger was obviously his age, but Omar looked older for some reason.

He had definitely grown up faster than most 14-year-old boys.

Case stood next to him.

"Your 'backup'?" Slider asked.

Case nodded at Omar Grebes.

"Slider, I want you to meet Omar. He's a member of an organization I think you might want to become a part of —"

Slider cut him off. "No way! No! I'm the only one who'll look out for me now that Mikey's gone."

Smiling, Omar looked at Case. "You're right, Detective. He's obstinate."

"Say what?" Slider asked.

"It means stubborn —"

"I know what it means, punk," Slider shot back.

"Slider, you've got something inside you, a raw, natural talent and this piece of board knew it, amplified it. We can teach you how to hone it, control it. Use it for the betterment of mankind," Omar said.

"And who are 'we'?" he asked suspiciously.

"Us?" Omar said. "We're just here to help."

Slider looked over at Juliet for some kind of sign. She nodded and took his hand.

"I trust him," she said softly.

Slider shot a look over to Case.

"And what do you think, Detective?" Slider asked.

Case flipped over his lapel. A small pin of a globe surrounded by lightning bolts was clipped to the underside of his blazer.

"Like I said, we're all here to help." Case smiled.

Slider was silent. Sure, he was a class clown and a rebel, but he had never done anything really malicious or hurt anyone. Now, he wondered if this was what Mr. Greenberg, his Spanish teacher, had been trying to tell him.

Was this what nerdy adults called a crossroads?

Was this the point in his life where he had to shape up and fly right?

Eyes narrowing, Slider nodded.

"Fine, I'll go with you. But that guy —" He pointed in the general direction that Rodney skated off in.

"— he's *mine*," he finished.

Placing a hand on Slider's shoulder, Omar smiled.

"You're gonna have to wait in a long line for that one, pal."

Omar pulled a cell phone out of his pocket and tapped a button.

"Bring her in," he said.

A blinding white light shined overhead as a sleek Black Hawk helicopter suddenly appeared.

The four of them shielded their eyes from the flying dust and dirt as the chopper landed in front of them.

"Do me a favor," Juliet said as she pulled on Slider's hand.

"What's that?" he asked.

She leaned in and kissed him softly. He was shocked at first, but he quickly relaxed and kissed her back.

As they pulled apart, she looked him in the eyes. "Be careful," she whispered.

"I will," he answered.

Stepping up, Case shook Slider's hand.

"Good luck, kid. Don't worry about your foster parents. We'll take good care of them. And don't worry about Rodney and those other guys. We'll look after Juliet and her family, too."

"And my brother?" he asked.

"We'll keep looking," answered Case. "I promise."

Nodding, Slider looked over at Juliet and smiled. "I'll see you soon."

They turned and walked toward the chopper.

"First kiss, huh?" Omar said.

"Shut it."

"She your girlfriend?" Omar asked.

"What's it to you?" Slider said.

"She's cute, that's all." Omar smiled.

"Are you always this nosey?" Slider said.

"You always this defensive?" Omar frowned.

"Only to people who can't mind their own business," Slider said.

Omar jumped on the chopper and offered a hand to Slider. He didn't take it.

"We're a team here, Slider, kinda like a family. I know that's new to you, but we take care of each other." Omar offered his hand again.

Slider looked at him, and looked at his hand.

A family. It's all he'd ever wanted.

Reaching up, Slider took Omar's hand and climbed onboard.

"Just stay out of my personal life," said Slider. He looked around and saw the other kids in the bird. *What is all this?* he wondered.

The door to the Black Hawk slammed shut. The rotors began picking up speed. Finally, the chopper lifted into the air as Slider looked out the porthole window in the door.

Below, Juliet and Detective Case stood watching them go. Juliet waved goodbye. She grew smaller and smaller as the helicopter rose into the air.

Slider looked around the cabin. There were three other kids in the chopper, two boys and a girl.

They smiled and nodded, silently welcoming him. He nodded back, but he was a little nervous about what his future held for him.

He looked at his hand, where the blue electricity had flowed through him. He felt at ease, like everything was going to be fine.

Omar smiled as they buckled in.

"Welcome to the family, Slider," he said. "Welcome to the *Revolution*."

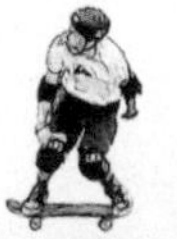

DYLAN CROW_
CODE NAME: SLIDER

AGE: 14

HOMETOWN: New York City

SPORT: Skateboarding

INTERESTS: Hip-hop, the Yankees, gaming

BIO: When you skate in New York, it's all about getting creative, and fourteen-year-old Dylan Crow considers himself a street artist. You won't catch him tagging the alley walls like some of his friends; instead he paints the streets with his board. This stylish teen rarely hits the skate parks. He wants to be seen grinding rails in Brooklyn, doing ollies in Central Park, and launching kickflips in Midtown. He's heavily influenced by some of today's top young skaters, including Ryan Sheckler, Chris Cole,.and Paul Rodriguez. His smooth skating style matches his personal appearance, which is born in hip-hop and indie-rock music — cocked Yankees cap, graphic T-shirt, clean khakis, and custom kicks.

STORY SETTING: Urban Battleground

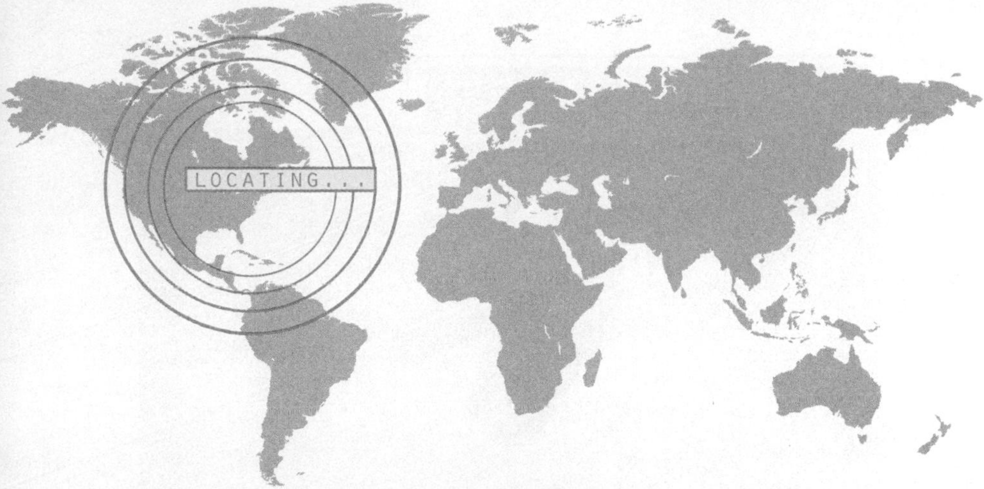
LOCATING...

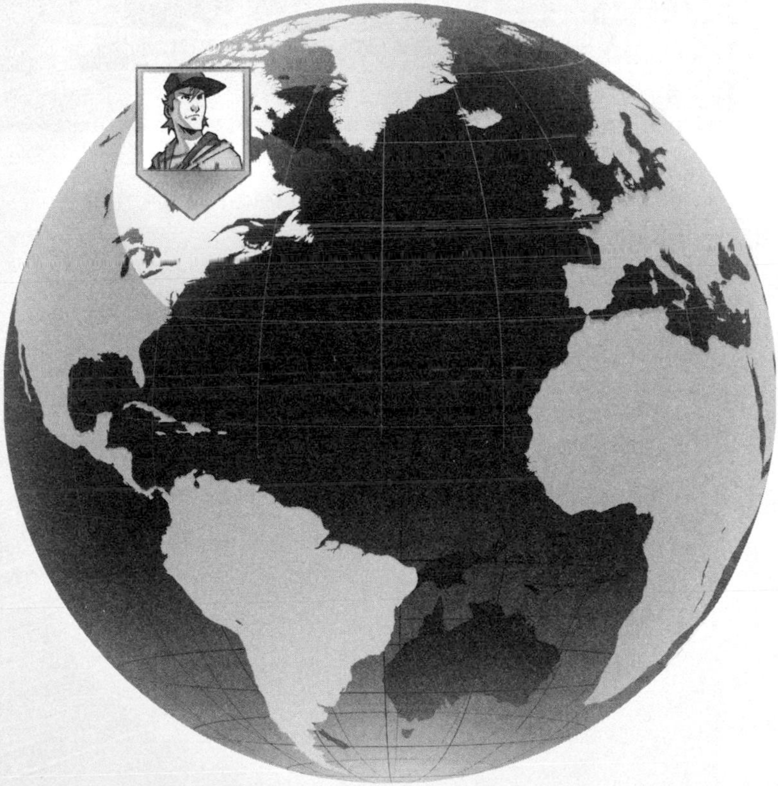

ABOUT TONY HAWK

TONY HAWK is the most famous and influential skateboarder of all time. In the 1980s and 1990s, he was instrumental in skateboarding's transformation from fringe pursuit to respected sport. After retiring from competitions in 2000, Tony continues to skate demos and tour all over the world.

He is the founder, President, and CEO of Tony Hawk Inc., which he continues to develop and grow. He is also the founder of the Tony Hawk Foundation, which works to create skateparks and empower youth in low income communitites.

TONY HAWK WAS THE FIRST SKATEBOARDER TO LAND THE 900 TRICK, A 2.5 REVOLUTION (900 DEGREES) AERIAL SPIN, PERFORMED ON A SKATEBOARD RAMP.

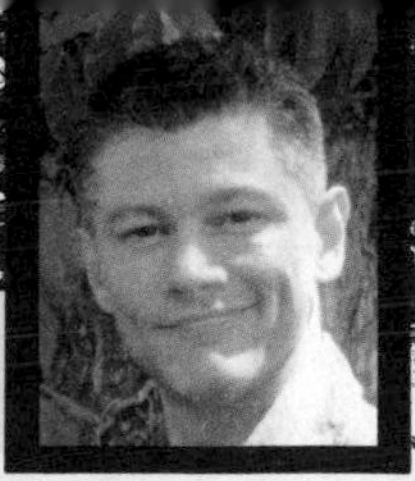

ABOUT THE AUTHOR_

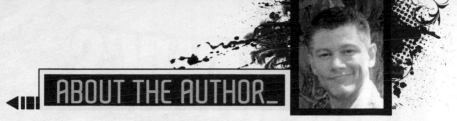

M. ZACHARY SHERMAN is a veteran of the United States Marine Corps. He has written comics for Marvel, Radical, Image, and Dark Horse. His recent work includes *America's Army: The Graphic Novel, Earp: Saint for Sinners,* and the second book in the *SOCOM: SEAL Team Seven* trilogy.

AUTHOR Q & A_

Q: When did you decide to become a writer?

A: I've been writing all my life, but the first professional gig I ever had was a screenplay for Illya Salkind (*Superman 1–3*) back in 1995. But it was a secondary profession, with small assignments here and there, and it wasn't until around 2005 that I began to get serious.

Q: Has your military experience affected your writing?

A: Absolutely, especially the discipline I have obtained. Time management is key when working on projects, so you must be able to govern yourself. In regards to story, I've met and been with many different people, which enabled me to become a better storyteller through character.

Q: What other projects have you worked on?

A: I've written several comic projects for companies like Marvel Comics and Image Comics, but I've also written screenplays for several movie projects that are this close to being made into films. And of course, video games like *SAW, Rogue Warrior,* and *America's Army.*

TONY HAWK'S 900 revolution

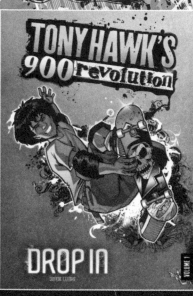

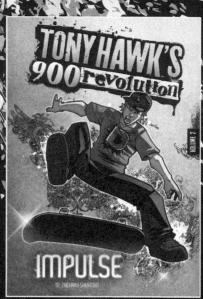

TONY HAWK'S
900 revolution
DROP IN
VOLUME 1

TONY HAWK'S
900 revolution
IMPULSE
VOLUME 2

TONY HAWK'S 900 REVOLUTION,
VOL. 1: DROP IN

Omar Grebes never slows down. When he's not shredding concrete at Ocean Beach Skate Park, he's kicking through surf or scarfing down fish tacos from the nearest roadside shop. Soon, his live-or-die lifestyle catches the attention of big-name sponsors. But one of them offers Omar more than he bargained for . . . a chance to become the first member of the mysterious 900 Revolution team and claim his piece of history.

TONY HAWK'S 900 REVOLUTION,
VOL. 2: IMPULSE

When you skate in New York, it's all about getting creative, and fourteen-year-old Dylan Crow considers himself a street artist. You won't catch him tagging alley walls. Instead, he paints the streets with his board. He wants to be seen grinding rails in Brooklyn and popping ollies at the Chelsea Piers. But when Dylan starts running with the wrong crowd, his future becomes a lot less certain . . . until he discovers the Revolution.

QUEST CONTINUES...

TONY HAWK'S
900 revolution
FALL LINE
VOLUME 3

TONY HAWK'S 900 REVOLUTION,
VOL. 3: FALL LINE

Amy Kestrel is a powder pig. Often hidden beneath five layers of hoodies, this bleach-blonde, CO ski bum is tough to spot on the street. However, get her on the slopes, and she's hard to miss. Amy always has the latest and greatest gear. But when a group of masked men threaten her mountain, she'll need every ounce of the one thing she lacks — confidence — and only the Revolution can help her find it.

TONY HAWK'S
900 revolution
VOLUME 4
UNCHAINED

TONY HAWK'S 900 REVOLUTION,
VOL. 4: UNCHAINED

Joey Rail learned to ride before he could walk. He's tried every two-wheeled sport imaginable, but he's always come back to BMX freestyle. The skills required for this daring sport suit his personality. Joey is an outdoor enthusiast and loves taking risks. But when he's approached by the first three members of the Revolution, Joey must make a decision . . . follow the same old path or take the road less traveled.

FALL LINE

. . . Jimmy picked up the pace as he shot down the mountain. Reaching the middle of the 15,000 foot slope, he took a quick visual inventory of the run — rocks, trees, moguls, dips, drifts, and possible jumps.

Snowboarding beside him, his friend Amy Kestrel felt a strange electrical energy crackling through her veins as she came down the decline. She pulled a toeside stop, shook her hands, and flexed her fingers, trying to get the warm blood circulating through them.

The static energy wouldn't stop. Every muscle in her body tingled with life. She felt indestructible.

Taking off her right glove, she looked down and examined her palms. A small amount of blue electricity arced and swam around her fingers, jumping from her painted nailtips like sparking metal conductors.

Eyes filled with wonder, Amy searched for Jimmy to show him the phenomenon, but he was too far ahead.

The teen didn't quite know what to do. Her confidence level was at an all-time high and, at that very moment, Amy Kestrel knew she could do anything she set her mind to.